HE

cheeseman
(BRP) FEB 2016
Patterson

2 2 FEB 2016

29 11 16 HE
7-1.2017

DISCARDED

D1376241

Books should be returned or renewed by the last
date above. Renew by phone **03000 41 31 31** or
online *www.kent.gov.uk/libs*

Libraries Registration & Archives

CUSTOMER
SERVICE
EXCELLENCE

CSE

Kent
County
Council
kent.gov.uk

C161018092

SPECIAL MESSAGE TO READERS

THE ULVERSCROFT FOUNDATION
(registered UK charity number 264873)

was established in 1972 to provide funds for
research, diagnosis and treatment of eye diseases.
Examples of major projects funded by
the Ulverscroft Foundation are:-

- The Children's Eye Unit at Moorfields Eye Hospital, London
- The Ulverscroft Children's Eye Unit at Great Ormond Street Hospital for Sick Children
- Funding research into eye diseases and treatment at the Department of Ophthalmology, University of Leicester
- The Ulverscroft Vision Research Group, Institute of Child Health
- Twin operating theatres at the Western Ophthalmic Hospital, London
- The Chair of Ophthalmology at the Royal Australian College of Ophthalmologists

You can help further the work of the Foundation
by making a donation or leaving a legacy.
Every contribution is gratefully received. If you
would like to help support the Foundation or
require further information, please contact:

THE ULVERSCROFT FOUNDATION
The Green, Bradgate Road, Anstey
Leicester LE7 7FU, England
Tel: (0116) 236 4325

website: www.foundation.ulverscroft.com

THE SUNDOWN RUN

Yancey Wade needed money, badly, and joining up with Frank Greer's wild bunch seemed the quickest way. But with Greer's plans to rob the Sundown Run — a legendary transport whose stagecoaches carry a fortune in gold ingots and bristle with shotgun guards — Wade soon discovers it is also the riskiest. Though many have tried, nobody has ever successfully robbed the Sundown Run before. But he has no choice — do it, or pay the ultimate price . . .

Books by Hank J. Kirby
in the Linford Western Library:

HELLFIRE PASS
BLOOD KIN
TRAVIS QUINN, OUTLAW
THE COUGAR CANYON RUN
COUNT YOUR BULLETS
MADIGAN'S LADY
NEVADA HAWK
FIND MADIGAN!
BOTH SIDES OF THE LAW
ONCE A RANGER
MONTANA MANHUNT
DRAGONFIRE TRAIL
HANGTREE COUNTY
THE LAST MANN
THE SCATTERGUN GANG
AGAINST ALL ODDS
NOT A HOPE IN HELL

HANK J. KIRBY

◆

THE SUNDOWN RUN

Complete and Unabridged

LINFORD
Leicester

First published in Great Britain in 2013 by
Robert Hale Limited
London

First Linford Edition
published 2015
by arrangement with
Robert Hale Limited
London

Copyright © 2013 by Hank J. Kirby
All rights reserved

A catalogue record for this book is available
from the British Library.

ISBN 978–1–4448–2393–6

Published by
F. A. Thorpe (Publishing)
Anstey, Leicestershire

Set by Words & Graphics Ltd.
Anstey, Leicestershire
Printed and bound in Great Britain by
T. J. International Ltd., Padstow, Cornwall

This book is printed on acid-free paper

KENT
ARTS & LIBRARIES

Prologue

New Mexico – 1878

It was too small a job to involve so many. That was Yancey Wade's opinion and he told Frank Greer in so many words, with a couple of epithets thrown in about wasting the gang's time for good measure.

Frank, big and brash, long black hair hanging to his shoulders, sucked at his bottom lip — one of his irritating habits — and shook his head slowly.

'Yance, you just dunno what you're talking about.'

'I know what I see — and that's a two-room shack at the edge of a jerk-water town with a stageline that only runs when the owner's sober enough to organize it. Even then it carries not much more than a load of groceries or mail orders for the poor benighted folk out

1

there on the plains — which, by the way, must knock hell out of that wreck of a stagecoach.'

'That's what you see, Yance. And what you see is what's there.' Frank took out the makings and began to build a cigarette with his thick fingers, not looking at Wade as he did so. 'Right along with what you *don't* see.'

'Frank, I'm in no mood for damn riddles! We're sitting out here on this knoll, the whole damn bunch of us, plain as day, and though that's a dump of a place, it does have a sheriff who once had a reputation as one helluva town-tamer. But I hear he don't even bother getting outta bed some mornings these days. Not if the bottle's within reach.'

'Aaaah! It's old bullet wounds that laid him low,' Frank said, firing up his smoke. 'Landers is still tough and he can call up a bunch of deputized townsfolk right smartly if he needs to.'

'Well, ain't that just one more reason to forget this damn stupid idea you had while you were in the privy?'

Frank's hooded eyes narrowed even more and he looked around at the other five men, silently sitting their mounts.

'Anyone sidin' with Yancey?'

A lot of shuffling and murmuring and dropping of gazes, but no clear answer from anyone. Frank spat.

'Yeah. Never could make up your own minds. Which is why I'm the leader. Now, look: Yancey's right in what he says — except for one thing. Because it's a jerkwater dump it don't mean there ain't a good haul in that Express office safe.'

'That stageline wouldn't be trusted to carry anything to make it worth our while bustin' in,' said Quinn, short of stature, wide of shoulder and mean as a rattler when he had a few redeyes under his belt, like now.

Frank was growing tired of this and demonstrated it with one of his other annoying habits: he crushed out his burning cigarette in the palm of his left hand, dusting off the shredded, still smouldering tobacco while he looked at his gang one by one.

'I'm still the boss,' he murmured in a low, menacing tone. 'You want to change that — then you know what you gotta do to get it done.'

He dropped a hand to his gun butt and the others tensed. No one made a move towards their own weapons. That seemed to satisfy Frank Greer and his thick lips moved in a crooked smile. 'Then, seein' as I have your trust, gents, let's go get what's in that safe.'

'You *know* for sure it's worthwhile?' Yancey Wade persisted, and stiffened as Frank snapped his head round, face set like a thunderhead ready to spit lightning.

'You — trust — me,' Frank said doggedly. 'Or — go for your gun and die right here.'

Wade shook his head slowly. 'I ain't keen on risking my hide in this dump, and I sure ain't stupid enough to risk my neck over what might or might not be there by goin' for my gun.'

'Wise decision.' Frank glared coldly, then gave a jerky nod. 'OK — let's go. You'll be mighty glad you did, I swear!'

It was late afternoon and Wade would have preferred to wait another hour, just to be on the safe side. He hadn't said so, but he'd tangled with the town's sheriff before. He might seem wore-out and a boozer now, but Wade had seen him in his prime and he knew a man only one year into retirement didn't lose his quick nor his courage in that time; not when he had nursed it along for more that thirty years behind a badge.

If he could be sure there was a good take in the Express safe, OK, but risking his neck for no more than drinking money didn't appeal.

But now it was too late.

They were already spreading out according to plan and someone in the Express office was lighting the lamps.

One thing about Frank: he made damn sure each man knew his job so he could do it in his sleep. Bugs Tyrell was already dismounting and heading for the alley alongside the clapboard building, tossing his reins in Shorty's direction. Quinn was next and Shorty passed quickly from man to man as they quit leather. They led their horses into the second alley — the one that Frank had found led to the rear of the Express building. Then they crossed three yards of open grass into a stand of trees — now dark with inky shadows. Perfect for the getaway.

'All right! Bandannas up. Make sure you're properly masked and let's get it done!'

There was no finesse about their entrance.

Frank kicked the door in. The Express man was just in the act of bending down to drop the door bolt into the floor, locking up for the night. The doors crashed into him and split his scalp open so that blood ran into his mouth as he yelled.

He was hurled halfway across the lamplit area in front of the counter, where an old woman stood counting receipts or money. Startled, her wrinkled face draining of all blood, she took in the scene in a flash. Grey hair swirled as she stooped and straightened much faster than anyone would expect of someone her age, lifting a shotgun. She fired as soon as it was clear of the counter-top. The one they called the Indian because he was one-eighth Cherokee, was lifted off his feet and slammed bloodily into Tex Lyle; they went down together, only Tex struggling.

'You damned old bitch!' yelled Frank in one of his rare moments of pure rage. His rifle butt was rammed against his hip and his hand blurred as he worked the lever again and again, pumping two bullets into the frail old lady. Her thin body twisted jerkily under the strike of lead. Even when she fell to the floor, Frank leaned over the counter and put one more bullet into her.

Wade's hand gripped his shoulder and spun him round; then he slammed his left fist into the middle of Greer's startled face. Frank's knees buckled and he went down halfway, bandanna mask half-off now.

'This is the last time I work with you, Frank!'

Greer drove the smoking rifle barrel into Wade's midriff. 'You — could — be right!'

Yancey grunted, gasping for breath. He thought he was dead, as Frank levered another shell into the breech of the rifle. Then Greer said between his teeth: 'You're s'posed to be openin' the doors of the cupboard where they hide the safe, goddammit! Now — get — to it!'

A mite dazed from the jab with the rifle barrel, which was still only two inches from his heart, Wade nodded, and went around the counter, stepping over the dead woman without looking at her. He fired his six-gun twice into the padlocked green door that hid the safe, metal buckling, wood splintering.

'All yours, Frank.'

But Greer used too much nitro on the heavy, brown-painted iron door and it wrecked half the counter. As the smoke cleared, Bugs Tyrell, waiting outside, stepped out of the alley mouth, a six-gun in each hand. The sheriff came stumbling up with a sawn-off 12-gauge shotgun swinging in one hand, looking only half-awake.

'Hey, Sher'ff. I think someone's robbin' the Express office.' Bugs pointed with his right-hand Colt towards the doors that had been splintered and blown across the boardwalk.

The lawman, startled, staggered as he tried to stop and swing towards the masked Tyrell. The sawed-off weapon lifted pretty damn fast in the rheumatic hands of a half-drunk seventy-year-old. But it never fired.

Tex Lyle pumped three bullets into him, then stood there, wreathed in gun-smoke, and watched the once-famous old lawman die in the dust of this no-account town.

People were running out of houses

and stores by now, but anyone who had a gun out — or even thought of getting one out — hastily ducked back inside as they saw their sheriff's blood-spattered figure huddled in the street and men with guns in their hands pouring out of the Express office. Shorty came running with the horses and Frank tossed a large leather drawstring pouch at him.

'*Vamoose!* Take that trail I showed you. We'll get our own mounts — and *you* better be waitin'at the camp when we get there. With the satchel.'

Suddenly there were gunshots from up the street and four men came bursting out of the town's one saloon, shooting at the dispersing gang. These were trail herders, in for a couple of quick drinks and some female company, and not about to stand still while this little town they'd found to be mighty hospitable was hoorawed.

The outlaws returned fire and one of the trail men spilled off the boardwalk into the gutter. The others ducked for cover but started shooting again as soon as they found it.

By then the gang was mounted and scattering. Wade swung his horse around the back and found Shorty sagging in the saddle, clutching his left side. Blood oozed between his fingers and the small man looked at him with real terror in his wide eyes above his bandanna. 'I — I'm done, Wade. Here . . .'

As he toppled from the saddle Shorty swung the leather drawstring bag that Frank had thrown him. Wade grabbed at it instinctively. Shorty hit the ground and lay there on his back, eyes wide and frozen in the death stare. Wade swore: he'd liked Shorty.

'Gimme that if you don't want it!'

Wade snapped his head up as Quinn came sweeping in on his horse and snatched the leather pouch from him. His other hand came down with a blazing six-gun. Wade ducked along his mount's neck, felt it shudder as the lead took it in the head. It started to go down as

Quinn spurred away. Wade only managed to free one boot from the stirrups. His left leg remained hung up as the horse took him down, pinning him under. Then riders came thundering down the alley, guns at the ready.

1

California — 1880

The man-hunters shot him in the back, stole his horse and left him for dead in the hellish tangle of ranges known locally as Madwoman's Knot.

He truly believed he would die here in this desolation that all but the desperate or plumb loco avoided. No food, no water, no shelter and now no means of transport. The wound was painful, high in the left shoulder; his shirt was making squishy sounds, so he knew it was still bleeding.

Well, maybe he would die peacefully, slowly fade away into a coma from which there would be no awakening. There were worse ways to die — but, goddammit! he didn't want to die — not yet. He hadn't done much with his life and now, now that he had the big chance to show what he could do, had come *this*!

A lousy bullet in the back — and it hadn't even been meant for him.

His consciousness had been fast fading when the men who had shot him gathered around his sprawled body. One of them had cursed bitterly, nudging him roughly with a scuffed boot-toe.

'Christ! It ain't him! That damn black hoss he was forkin' throwed me off. Thought we had the son of a bitch.'

'Well, we might's well take the hoss and whatever cash he has on him and get the hell outta here,' said a second voice, rough, indifferent. 'Lend a hand, Bugs. There's a slew of weight in the sonuver.'

His groans had been loud as they rolled him over, pulled him this way and that, went through his pockets expertly. By then the pain was really getting to him and he was fading fast when he heard the rough voice, as if coming down a deep well:

'Not worth the effort. All his money's in letters of credit on different banks. *Shoot!*' He drove a boot solidly into the man's side. 'C'mon. We got a lotta time to make up.'

Flashes of pain took the semi-conscious man to strange places. He wasn't aware that he cried out several times. When things became a little clearer he lay there, breathing fast, eyeslids barely open, the sticky lashes blurring his vision. Alone.

Until he felt a strange, almost imperceptible coolness on his face, followed by the blocking-out of the searing sun. He forced his eyes open a little more, made out the blurred shape of a man standing over him, holding the reins of a dusty black gelding that looked mighty jaded.

'They put one into your back, eh? Lucky you were ridin' away or it might've blown your chest apart.' The man crouched over him. 'Had a look at the wound. Not good, but not fatal. If you can get to a doctor.' A hand waved

15

limply and the visitor's head moved slowly from side to side. 'No, not me, feller. I can't take you. Hoss is tuckered, couldn't carry the both of us and I need to be moving along.' He paused and added, 'To just about any place, as long as it's far from here.'

'Y-you — you're the — one they — want,' the wounded man gasped. 'Mistook — me — on a — a black horse, like — yours . . . '

'Yeah. Hard luck, for you.'

'Then — help — me . . . '

'Like to, *amigo*, but you heard what I said. My hoss can't carry us both. And I have priority. Tell you what, tho', I've got a mouthful of water left in my canteen. You're welcome to it. Er . . . you got any money, by the way?'

The wounded man jerked his head at the question, blinking, trying to get a better look at this no-good Samaritan. 'You — you're going to *sell* it to me? You — lousy . . . ' He thought the stranger's face looked strong, the jaw stubborn and, even crouching, he seemed tall. Nothing clearer . . . except steady grey eyes. Kind of man you might trust on looks — just goes to show!

'Mind if I look through your pockets?'

'As if . . . I could stop . . . you!'

He felt big hands going over his body, but more gently than those of the men who had shot him; they had found a couple of dollars and his letters of credit, but they hadn't found the coins in the linings of his boots' insoles . . .

Ah! Dammittohell! This one was more thorough.

The tall man straightened, jingling the coins. 'Four double eagles. Not bad. You give 'em for a mouthful of canteen water, friend?'

'I — I'd like to give you . . . a bellyful of buckshot!'

'Yeah. Savvy how you feel. But it's all a matter of me bein' kinda desperate and needing the gold more'n you. Won't do you no good way you are — or will be.'

'Christ! You're . . . cold! Gimme the water.'

It was tepid and flat and he spluttered some, prompting the tall man to say, 'Don't waste it!'

Gulping, the wounded man tried to glare but he was too weak. 'Never known a . . . sonofabitch . . . like you . . . '

'Aw, don't worry about it, friend. I don't mind you calling me names. I guess it ain't the right kinda treatment I'm giving you, but . . . circumstances, you know?' He put the coins in his pocket as he stood looking around. 'I'll move you into the shade of that brush up there make you a mite more comfortable.'

As he bent to get a grip on the man, the gasping voice said, querying, 'That a — posse — that's after you?'

The tall man's reply was very terse: 'No, it's not.' As he heaved again the wounded man swore with the pain and weakly pummelled him. But then he couldn't manage any more and through

18

a red haze he sensed himself lowered to the ground, felt the coolness of shade as the tall man arranged the brush around him after stuffing a balled-up kerchief over the wound.

'That'll hold you for a spell.'

'Y — you're just gonna leave me here . . . to die?'

'Hey, pard. I keep tellin' you: I can't take you with me. I been on the grubline a long time. Got nothing to doctor your wound. All I can do is make your passing a mite more — easy.' For the first time the wounded man noticed that this tall stranger walked with a limp, idly rubbed at his left hip occasionally.

'Just one Good Samaritan, aren't you?' He heard the creak of saddle leather as the man mounted the near-jaded black. 'Why the hell did you bother to even stop?' There was a trace of disgust in the dying man's voice.

'I was backshot once. Left to die in the middle of a wasteland. Just like you. Was an Injun saved me. When I seen

19

you — well, I figured it must be my turn to kinda square up.'

The wounded man was stunned by the words; when he turned his head again the man had gone from the ambit of his vision. 'This what you call . . . 'squarin' up'?'

A few words drifted back through the buzz of insects coming to investigate this newcomer to their territory.

'Good luck, *amigo*. You'll need all you can get.'

'Stick your luck!' It cost the wounded man plenty to make himself heard, but the rider reined down, turned the horse and rested folded hands on the saddle horn.

'Listen, pard, I need to get the hell outta here. I've nothing that can help you. Even had to — kinda — steal your money. No way I can do you any good. Can't you savvy that?'

'You got a six-gun rammed in your belt. Which . . . which has more empty loops than full. *Hey!* You — you aren't on the grubline! You — you're on the dodge! You're ducking the law. That was a posse that shot me!'

'They weren't law, friend.' Then there was a long silence broken only by the restless shifting of the weary horse's feet. 'I need all my bullets too. Anyway no point in . . . '

The rider shrugged, started to turn away, halted with a jerk that brought a grunt of disapproval from the gelding, as the hurt man *laughed*!

'Wasting them on a — dead man?'

'Pain gettin' to you, feller? You goin' loco?'

The harsh sound died. 'No! But you know, you've already killed a . . . dead man.'

'Save your breath.'

As the tall man started to turn the black again, the gasping voice said,

'Me! I'm a dead man. *Walt Dedman!* Ain't that a laugh? Dedman's a — dead man.'

2

Sundown

It bothered the tall rider, leaving a wounded man like that.

He told himself over and over there was just no choice, dammit. None! If Greer and Bugs Tyrell got their hands on him he would be left alone to die of his wounds — if they didn't shoot him to pieces a little at a time.

And that would be the best solution all round, leastways, from *their* point of view.

Walt Dedman. Poor, unlucky sonuver. Mebbe doomed from the day he was born into a name like that.

He shook himself roughly, causing the stumble-stepping black to stagger a little more, accompanied by a snort that was only half-hearted because the animal was plumb wore out from the long, five-day flight through some of the mean-est country he'd ever seen in this part of California.

And he wasn't out of it yet. *Just look around*, he thought, squinting with those hard grey eyes as the sun etched the desert rimrock with blinding fire.

Another hour or so 'til sundown. Time to clear this bushwhacker's country, maybe see the lights of a distant town. His fingers went to his shirt pocket involuntarily as he felt the weight of the gold coins dragging at the sweat-stained cloth.

'Damn!' he muttered. He had hated taking them. Then he chuckled shortly: hell, Yancey Wade, man with a con-science! Now who the hell in his right mind would believe that?'

That very instant something moved up there on the rim: just a suggestion of a ripple in the glare-line. Then he saw the rifle flash and heard the thumping passage of the bullet as it flicked hot air against his cheek. No thought to it: he left the saddle in a wild plunge,

23

snatching his rifle from the scabbard, seeing that he had instinctively chosen the side with some brush that would break his fall. Three more shots ripped into the brush, leaves and twigs erupting, before he hit the ground. Instincts still working at top speed, he spun away from a bush, kicking against its four-inch-thick stalk, propelling himself in the direction of another bush growing from a small clump of rocks, a few feet below.

As he slid and scrambled for the cover he glimpsed, out of the corner of his eye, the black sliding down and past him, belly scraping, weary legs working wildly. But it was smarter than he was: it clambered over a line of small boulders that were apparently big enough to give it protection from the bullets screaming around them both.

Wade levered, knowing there were only four shots left in the Winchester's magazine. He had to make them count.

The man above had been shooting continually all the time while Wade was

24

falling and throwing himself around amongst the brush. Two more shots ricocheted from the rocks below him, then came silence: the shooter would be desperately thumbing fresh cartridges into the loading gate. As if to confirm this there were three or four random flashes from up there on the rim: the sinking sun touching the brass sideplate of the rifle as the killer worked feverishly, jiggling the weapon in his efforts to reload.

Wade had been taking in the terrain as he crouched, still moving sideways and down, keeping rocks between him and the rim as best he could. There was a drop into a narrow cleft and he took it without hesitation. Crouching low, now without a choice, he felt the ground under him rising, and hunched even lower, back scraping the rock above, as he groped forward in semi-darkness.

The rifle muzzle dragged across a rock and two shots slammed into the overhang above him. He winced and tried to squeeze himself into a gap between two boulders as the lead ricocheted. His teeth were bared, his heart pounding at the thought of one of those flattened pieces of lead — likely now the size of a half-dollar — slicing into his body or taking the top off his skull like a buzz-saw.

Belly down, he got his scuffed boot-soles against a solid rock and heaved, legs straightening as if propelled on springs. He misjudged a little and his hat was knocked off as his head scraped the underside of a tilted boulder. Stars blinked briefly before his eyes and then he was twisting and grunting as he forced himself through the narrow opening, pushing the rifle ahead of him.

It waved erratically because he couldn't get a firm enough grip and this earned him another bullet, which came mighty close to his head. Then, without warning he was falling. He'd over-balanced in the dimness, not realizing that the rock he was crawling across had, aeons ago, snapped in half above a man-deep pocket in the rocks.

He tumbled into this, and found that there was coarse sand in the bottom, which cushioned his falling body. It looked as if rainwater from countless storms had channelled through here and, over the years, had cut a shallow, rising trough in the rock. There was no water now, and pre-sundown light filtered in, outlining the course, rising all the time.

Good enough. He slithered up like a snake, holding the rifle awkwardly, one thumb on the hammer sear, because he could now hear the man who was trying to kill him! He was cursing and changing position, boots slipping on gravel, the rifle clanging against a rock. But he didn't seem to care; he must have found what he figured to be a better spot, and was hurriedly making for it, before the light went.

The man's noise covered Wade's own efforts as he virtually surged up the under-rock channel, tensing some when it narrowed and he had to turn on his side, working elbows and knees awkwardly.

But then he emerged into dusk, not a dozen feet from where he could see the bushwhacker getting into position for shooting over the far edge.

The man must have heard him, spun around swiftly, shooting his rifle one-handed. The barrel leaped, throwing the bullet high. He levered rapidly and expertly, got off two more hurried shots before Yancey Wade shot him through the chest, knocking him down violently. Wade levered and swung the smoking barrel towards the wounded man.

'Got you dead to rights, feller! Your choice now.'

The man's face was twisted in agony, but there was raw hatred glowing in those dark eyes and he deliberately, though mighty awkwardly, jacked another shell into the breech, struggled to bring the rifle around.

'You always were a blamed fool, Curry!' Wade said softly, recognizing the bushwhacker now. He shot him through the head.

Wade crawled up to the dead man and checked him over visually. Yeah, it was Stew Curry all right: back-shooting bounty hunter who should have run out of luck long ago.

'Well, mebbe the Devil'll pay you a bounty for all the poor bastards you've bushwhacked.'

He crawled out of the rocks, surprised to see how light it still was once he was free of their shadows. He sat on a high boulder, making a cigarette, and glanced back towards the Madwoman's Knot country.

He could barely make out a kind of moving smudge in the sky, a thin shadow travelling in imperfect circles — just about above the place he had left Walt Dedman.

His tongue paused halfway along the edge of the cigarette paper as he realized what that 'smudge' was.

Vultures — dozens of them — hovering.

3

Rescued

Walt Dedman figured he must have died and somehow found his way to Heaven.

That was his first hazy thought as he opened his eyes, blinked them into focus, and saw the angel with the reddish halo standing a few feet away.

She was facing him — but concentrating on the tattered book she held: no doubt checking to see if he was listed on some celestial guest list.

He shook his head and gave a small grunt as he tried to clear his aching brain of such foolish thoughts.

There! It wasn't a red halo at all! Nor an angel.

Just a good-looking young woman, sunshine at the window behind her outlining her mop of chestnut hair, giving it a ruddy glow . . . like a halo.

She must have heard his grunt, for she snapped her head up, set the book aside on a nearby small table and came towards him, smiling warmly.

'Oh, you're conscious. Thank Heaven. I — I thought for a time there it was touch and go — mostly 'go', if you'll excuse my levity. It's just that I'm so glad you're going to be all right!'

He tried to speak but only guttural sounds came. She poured him a tumbler of water from a china ewer on a bedside table, and held his head while he swallowed a couple of mouthfuls.

Then he moaned and she lowered him back to the pillows.

'I'm sorry,' she said swiftly, contritely. 'I — didn't think. That must have put pressure on your wound, straining your neck like that.'

'Ma'am,' Dedman croaked, 'I — I'm mighty grateful that I can — feel such pain.' As she frowned, puzzled, he added: 'Means I — I'm not dead after all.'

She smiled and as she fussed with the bedsheets and fluffed the pillows, he saw she was in her mid-to-late twenties, skin fairly smooth, despite the deep tan from lots of outdoor exposure, he figured. She was wearing a checked shirt, corduroy trousers that were patched on one side, a trifle baggy. Standing upright, he reckoned she wouldn't be any taller than five feet four or five at the most — and she was wearing scuffed high-heel riding-boots, so you could drop a couple of inches off that estimate.

'We don't even know your name.' Her voice was pleasant enough and he felt her warm breath touch his cheek as she adjusted the pillows one more time. 'You weren't carrying any papers.'

He shook his head, half-smiling. 'Dunno your name, neither.

'Oh — well, I'm Mattie Groom. You're at my place in the southern part of the Sundown Ranges, part of the Inyo Mountains. It's just a small — *very* small — spread. And you are . . . ?'

'Nice to meet you, ma'am. I'm Walt Dedman.' He looked around the room, straining a little to see past her shoulder before she straightened.

'Is there something you want, Mr . . . Dedman?'

'I was wondering — where's the feller who must've brought me in?'

'I don't know. He left as suddenly as he appeared.' She looked into his pale, puzzled face.

'He found me . . . lying amongst the rocks, with the bullet in my back, where they'd left me.'

She straightened abruptly. ''They?' The people who shot you — abandoned you?'

He nodded. 'I thought they were a posse. Mistook me for someone else. You heard of a posse working this area?'

'No-ooo, not lately. Though the occasional one passes through on its way deeper into the range.' She paused, added quietly: 'On their hunt for fugitives.'

She thought he was going to say

something but he apparently changed his mind, so she continued:

'All I can tell you is that this man rode in here night before last with you roped to an old saddle on what we believe must have been a packhorse. He spoke to Jason, my brother, said he'd found a wounded man and he wanted to leave him here while he rode on into town and arranged for a doctor to come out to attend to him. I don't believe he mentioned his name but he certainly saw Doctor Pettigrew in Eton's Creek, who eventually came out here to tend you.'

Her smile twisted slightly. 'In fact, he told the doctor I'd sent him in because one of my men had had an accident and needed urgent attention. A lie, but a smart one. It got Doc Pettigrew moving a lot faster than normal.'

She let her words drift off as she saw his face: it was obvious that Walt Dedman had been thinking of something else while she was trying to explain how he came to be here.

'He was tall and fair-haired, stubbled and had obviously done some hard riding recently. I remember his eyes mostly. They were grey — reminded me of sheet steel.'

'By damn!' he breathed suddenly. 'He came back for me!' He looked straight into the girl's eyes and said, 'I — sensed he wasn't really the type to abandon a wounded man. I . . . I thought I was dreaming when someone chased the vultures away and took me from under the bushes where he'd left me. I vaguely remember him straining to lift me onto a horse and rope me in place.'

'Your mysterious friend did more than that. He washed and bandaged your shoulder, using an old shirt to hold rags over the wound to help stop the bleeding. Dr Pettigrew said you could have easily bled to death otherwise.'

'And you don't know where he is now?'

'I've no idea. He could be still in town — or maybe he's moved on. He didn't come back with the doctor.'

35

Dedman nodded. 'He'll have moved on. He had to keep going, he told me.' He sighed. 'Well, one day I hope he stays still long enough for me to thank him for saving my life.'

'He certainly did that; he's one of those rare individuals we call a Good Samaritan.'

'I once thought of him as a no-good Samaritan.' She looked at him sharply but all he said was: 'He only had a jaded black gelding when he found me. It couldn't carry us both, which is why he left me under the brush.'

'But didn't he attend to your wound, first?'

Dedman shook his head. 'He had nothing he could use to help me, not even a bandage. So he must've gotten another horse from somewhere; when he left he was riding a mighty weary black but I recall he was on a claybank after he got me roped on to the other horse — and I know for a fact he never even had a spare shirt when he first found me.'

'I — I'm not sure what you're trying to explain, Mr Dedman.'

'Call me Walt. No, well, it hardly matters now. I guess he had a conscience I didn't give him credit for after all.'

She looked puzzled, maybe a little annoyed, but he merely smiled crook-edly.

'Well, that's something between him and me, ma'am. No doubt it'll be sorted out some time. How long you think I'll be here?'

'I don't know. The doctor says you'll likely have a permanently stiff shoulder. But you're welcome to stay for as long as it takes to get you on your feet properly again. Is there someone you'd like me to notify that you've been hurt?'

'N-n-n-no, ma'am. Not right now. I was on my way to a new job but I'd've been arriving early, so with luck I'll still get there on time. Not sure I'll be able to pay the doctor, though. I — er — lost what money I had.'

'Oh! I think that's been taken care of.

Doc Pettigrew mentioned that your mysterious benefactor left a double eagle with him to cover his fees.'

'Well, I'll be double-damned!'

She waited in vain for him to elaborate, then compressed her lips a mite irritably and prepared to leave the room when he didn't.

'I'll bring you some food.'

'Just some coffee, if you don't mind, Mrs Groom. I'll eat later.'

'Coffee then — and it's *Miss* Groom. I run this place with my brother, Jason. But we can talk about those things later.'

Walt Dedman nodded, feeling suddenly weary, but even as he started to doze a little, he murmured,

'He came back for me. Must've risked his neck to do it. And the names I called him when he left me! Mister, I sure hope we meet again.'

But by that time it was just a thought wandering through his spinning brain and he began to snore gently, groaning a little as he tried to hitch into a more comfortable position.

That shoulder was sure damn painful.

He hoped it wouldn't stop him taking up the job he'd been hired for.

But that was something to worry about later.

4

Ridin' Shotgun

It was ideal country for a hold-up and as Yancey Wade took a firmer grip on the iron seat-arm, jolting as the stagecoach hit a pothole, he cursed when his hat tilted forward slightly, obscuring his vision.

'You need to get some eyeglasses, Zeke,' he shouted to the driver, his words fighting the hot wind. 'Might see them potholes before you drive down into one and get us lost.'

The driver was a man in his fifties. His jaws were working a wad of tobacco. He grinned at Wade beside him, showing stained teeth, before shooting a brown stream between the rumps of the straining horses in the rear of the team.

'Now you know why I brought that

extra blanket with me.' He gestured to the folded grey woollen blanket he was sitting on, and winked knowingly. 'Comes with maturity.'

'Might've warned me.'

'All you had to do was ask what the trail was like and — *Holy Joe!*'

This last was shouted in surprise and brought Zeke half-rising out of his seat as he hauled on the six-in-hand reins powerfully enough to pull the team leaders' heads up, snorting and writhing.

Wade tightened his grip on the seat arm, juggled the shotgun in his other hand as they rounded the bend and saw the three big rocks almost entirely blocking the trail.

'Go left! Go left!' he yelled. 'Don't stop! Jesus, Zeke, are you deaf as well as blind? *Left!* It's a trap!'

Even as he spoke and Zeke belatedly hauled left on the reins there came a volley of shots, just audible above the roar of the wind and the rattle of the stagecoach.

The two lead horses went down, headshot, and then it was a crazy series of jolts and blurred vision as the rest of the team piled into the tumbling bodies and the stage rode up over the backs of the rear horses. The vehicle shuddered and wood splintered, the shrill screams of the animals cut through the sounds of wreckage piling up and the startled, panicky yells of the three passengers bouncing around inside.

Wade leapt wildly, kicking away from the tilting vehicle, almost somersaulting in midair. Zeke went the other way, but being older and a sufferer from rheumatics, did not clear the stage completely. He yelled as his left lower leg slid between the blurred spokes of the front wheel and the bone snapped like a dead match. His body was dragged and bounced for several yards before the coach fell on its side, spun halfway round, and lay in a swirling cloud of dust.

Yancey Wade had managed to hold on to the shotgun, had had the breath knocked out of him and had collected a couple of dozen bruises and bumps, but he was still functioning; he rolled onto his belly, fumbling to cock the Greener.

He spat grit, blinked his eyes rapidly, trying to clear them of dust particles. There were blurred movements to his left and he swung that way, fired one barrel. A man yelled and one of the blurs fell away to ground level. Bullets stitched a short, ragged line in front of Wade's face. He winced as gravel raked his cheeks and forehead. His hat had gone during the fall and his long fair hair whipped in the breeze as he sought another target. He triggered the second barrel in the general direction of the movement he had seen, dropped the empty weapon and dragged his six-gun from his holster.

He heard rapid footfalls, then a rifle muzzle prodded roughly against the back of his neck, forcing his face into the ground.

'Still quick on the trigger, huh, Yancey?' a rough voice said above him as he opened his hand and let the Colt fall.

43

He half-twisted onto his side, squinted at the big man towering above him. He lifted one hand to shade his eyes.

'Might've known it was you, Frank. First the rocks that looked like they could've fallen naturally, then shooting the lead team broncs. You never did respect horseflesh.'

'It's all right for eatin' when you can't get beef,' Frank Greer grated in that gravelly voice. 'Ask any Injun. So, we finally ran you down, Yancey.'

'They just know me as 'Wade' here.'

'That so? Well, *I* know you as the son of a bitch who ran off with my share of the take from the Reno Creek Express office. Just over a year back now. Recollect?'

He emphasized the last word with a brutal kick to Wade's side. The shotgun guard groaned as his body skidded a good twelve inches with the impact. Face contorted with pain, Wade looked into Greer's rugged, dirt-smeared features, his thick lips curling under the ragged moustache he now sported.

Wade glared. 'I didn't steal it. Quinn grabbed it after shooting my hoss. My leg was pinned under.'

Greer moved his big head slowly, shoulder-length jet-black hair flying briefly. 'You sure do have some bad luck with hosses, don't you?'

'Quinn meant to shoot me!'

'Well, he never was much of a shot. But you must've gotten out from under the hoss behind that Express office. Last we seen was a bunch of riders headin' up that alley. They'd've found you if you was still pinned.'

Wade nodded, remembering. 'I played dead. Was them trail herders. One of 'em must've gone into the office and found the old woman. He yelled and they all dismounted, ran in to look.' He paused, eyes cold.

Frank shrugged. 'Stupid old biddy. Reminded me of my mother. She used to whip me with a knotted rope and — '

'One bullet would've been enough, Frank, if you had to shoot her at all!

45

Right then I figured to quit the gang, worked my leg free, and grabbed one of the herders' mounts. Never did catch up with Quinn, though.'

'We found his hoss dead, at the foot of Ponytail Rapids. But the saddle-bags were empty.'

'Surprise, surprise,' panted Wade. 'And I bet you never found Quinn's body. Right?'

Frank's milky-blue eyes narrowed and he raised his boot again but chuckled when Wade instinctively winced and curled into a ball. 'Ah. If Quinn'd been ridin' that hoss across the river and got caught in the rapids, his body could've been washed miles downstream.'

'Don't tell me you didn't look.'

'We looked, even dragged a coupla pools. Found his hat was all. No loot.'

'So you figured I must've took it — and came after me.' Wade shook his head slowly, wary of that rifle, watching the knuckle of Frank's trigger finger. 'You've had me on the run for a damn long time, Frank! Even sent that

46

half-wit Stew Curry to nail me. At least I got his horse, but I'm still telling you: *I didn't take that Express money!*'

Greer was silent while Wade looked around and saw the rest of the old gang, ignoring their dead comrade while they looted the stage's wreckage and went through the clothes of the unconscious passengers — two women and a man.

'Who'd I get with the shotgun? Dexter?'

'Yeah. No loss. What you got in that Express box?' Frank asked suddenly, pointing to the ironbound box canted on its side against a bush. 'You musta been guardin' somethin'.'

Wade bared his teeth. 'Mostly Zeke's and my lunch. This is a decoy run, Frank. Got mebbe fifty dollars in nickels and dimes, change for the general store in Lacey. The payroll you were expectin' us to be carrying went through last night, transferred to the Mormon wagon train.'

Frank was not pleased and the dusty

faces of the other outlaws who had come up, hardened. 'Lemme shoot off a couple of his toes, Frank,' pleaded Bugs Tyrell. 'I'll get the truth outta him.'

'Me, too,' growled Tex Lyle, drawing his big hunting-knife. But Wes Toohey, oldest of the wild bunch spat and said, 'Wade ain't joshin'. He rode with us long enough for you to know that. Me, I never did figure he double-crossed us. Quinn, yeah, I can believe that. Doubt we'll ever see that sonuver again, though.'

Frank glared at his men and his boot nudged Wade roughly in the ribs again. 'For now, we'll let it rest. But we will come back to it, you can take that as gospel.' He squatted suddenly, close to Wade's head. 'Been playin' the Good Samaritan again, too, ain't you?'

Wade frowned, but tensed up in his belly. 'Me?'

'You!' Frank clouted Wade across the head casually. 'You were always too damn soft. Thought we had you dead to rights a while back, but feller we nailed

48

just happened to be ridin' a hoss same colour as yours. But you know all about that, don't you?'

'How would I?'

Frank hit him across the mouth, leaned closer. 'Told you, you can't help playin' the Good Samaritan. *Reno Chronicle* had an article about a feller named Walt Dedman. Somethin' of a big shot now, workin' for that new Sundown Stageline. *He* was the one we mistook for you, put a bullet in his back, left him when we realized our mistake. But someone who shall, for the moment, remain nameless, found him, got him to a sawbones, and he pulled through. He didn't even know the do-gooder's name. Just had a rough description: tall, thirties, not bad-lookin', with grey eyes, like cold steel. Your kinda eyes.'

'Me — and a hundred others.'

Another swipe across the mouth. 'You're the only one *I* know, and we'd trailed you to that area where Dedman was shot by mistake. It was you saved his neck, all right.'

'Well, s'pose that's so? What difference does it make now?'

Frank grinned. 'You'd be surprised. This Dedman talked to the *Reno Chronicle* reporter. He wants to find you. Reward you for savin' his life. Don't that bring tears to your eyes?'

'Not mine.'

'How about this?'

Frank's boots beat a painful tattoo on Wade's supine body and the others were quick to join in. He tried to cover as best he could, but his arms were kicked and stomped on, too. He thought his head was going to come loose from his neck. Blood poured into his mouth from his battered nostrils, blinded him from cuts above both eyes.

Then, suddenly, he had someone's boot between his hands. He yanked and twisted savagely. He thought it was Tex Lyle who yelled and fell sprawling. But then they were all over him again and he left the scene in a red haze that all too slowly merged into pain-throbbing blackness.

* * *

They brought him round with hard
slaps and splashes of warm canteen
water, which, even blood-flavoured, felt
mighty good on his parched throat. One
eye was swollen so he could hardly see.
His jaw ached and his body — well, he
felt like someone had thrown him off a
cliff.

They had dragged him into the shade
of some rocks now and he looked
around, started to feel a terrible
coldness in his belly.

'Where's the stage?' he slurred, then
Frank Greer appeared in front of him,
kneeling over him now.

'Back a ways, where it crashed. Your
driver's in a bad way. Passengers are
shook up to hell but they'll make it.
They figure you've gone for help. See
what a do-gooder reputation does for
you?' He pushed Wade's battered head
roughly. 'So we'll take you someplace
close to where you really can get help
for 'em. Gotta keep up that rep, eh?'

'The hell're you up to, Frank?'

Greer's face sobered. 'Told you: Dedman's real keen to find you and re-ward you for helping him.'

'It happened over a year ago. Anyway, I don't want — '

Frank slapped him across already swollen, cut lips. 'Don't matter what *you* want, *amigo*. It's what we want.'

Wade spat some blood. 'Which is . . . ?'

'Walt Dedman's runnin' a new way station at Sundown Ridge. We're in Sundown country here: mountains, ridges, cricks, most every damn thing's got 'Sundown' in the name. Anyways, this way station's a big new place, where the stages can turn around, make repairs, pick up fresh teams, feed the payin' passengers. Even got rooms for sleep-overs and so on. You likely heard about it. It's a big deal for out here.'

Wade nodded, eyes bleak and deadly despite the swelling and bruises. Every-one knew about that fancy swing station: pride of the Sundown Stageline: 'Sunup To Sundown. Every Day Of The Week!'

'Place is built on land that used to be owned by some gal and her brother, named Groom. Seems it was their place you took Dedman to and then sent a sawbones out to doctor him. The woman, Mattie Groom, nursed Dedman back to health and he talked the stageline into buyin' the ridge off her and buildin' the way station. Very picturesque, gives the passengers their money's worth. She never had used half of her land, 'cause she couldn't afford a big enough herd to make it worthwhile. Now Dedman's fixed it so she can build up a decent spread, all because she helped him when he needed it! Now, feller like that'd be almighty pleased to see the man who brung him in from that wasteland, don't you reckon? Sure he would. He'd bend over backwards to give that lucky sonofabitch just about anythin' he wanted.'

'What would this lucky do-gooder want, Frank?'

'Aw, maybe a job on the Sundown Stageline, likely. You know, head shotgun guard, chief wrangler, makin' sure the change-over teams are all nice an' gentle an' ready at the way stations. Mebbe even a shippin' agent's job: somethin' with responsibility so's he'd get good pay — and know what's goin' on with the stageline. Dedman could swing all them things easy. He's a pretty important feller.'

'Uh-huh. It's possible, I guess. But s'pose I don't want 'em?'

Frank smiled widely, a genuine eye-lighting smile: the first Wade had ever seen him give, in all the years he'd known the man. ''Course you want 'em. Take my word for it.'

Yancey frowned, wondering if it would even be noticed among the swellings and cuts on his battered face.

'I don't get this, Frank.'

'Then listen. Ever heard of what they call the Sundown Run? Aw, come on, Yancey! Even ridin' shotgun on this jerkwater stageline you're with now, you must know what I mean.'

Wade's insides turned cold. *He couldn't be serious!*

54

'Forty-five, fifty thousand dollars' worth of refined gold, shipped out by the Fiddler's Green Mining Company every month or six weeks or so. Random times, never use the same route twice.' Wade murmured it, and noticed the tightness now around the edges of Frank's smile.

'See? You know about it all right! Guess which stageline's got the contract for carryin' all that bright yaller stuff this year? Ah! You know what I'm about, huh?'

'I know it's the best and tightest-guarded run in this territory. Never been robbed successfully. The route's kept secret right till the last minute and — '

'Yeah, yeah, all that kinda stuff. Only guards with top reputations, fast, crack shots, Bible-bangers, or at least upstandin' citizens. Paid damn well so it wouldn't be worth 'em tryin' a double-cross, anyways. All to be expected when they're handlin' so much dinero. I know all that stuff!'

'So what's the use of even thinking

about robbing that stage?'

'Aw, it'd be plain stupid for someone to try. *Unless* they had information that guaranteed they *would* get their hands on that gold.' He spread his arms. 'What're friends for, huh?'

Wade looked at him coldly now; he'd caught up with Frank's reasoning and the way those eyes burned in the battered, bloody face, made even Greer's belly give a jump or two. 'You and me were never friends, Frank.'

'Mebbe not, but we tolerated each other. In our business that's about as close as you come to makin' friends.' Then Greer leaned down. 'Most folk'd agree with you about what a hard job it'd be to rob that special stage, but you're gonna help me prove 'em wrong.'

'What makes you think so?'

'Well, I could turn you in to the law and pick up a miserable bounty. Could even shoot you first — you're wanted *dead or alive* in Arizona, you know.' He suddenly paused and clicked his fingers. 'Hey! Talkin' of *Arizona*! I seem to recollect a five- or six-year-old boy back there in a town called — what's its name again?' He waited and grinned tightly at Wade's suddenly grey face. 'Ah, it's just come to me: Montville, little ways north of Flagstaff. He's a nice kid, the one I'm talkin' about: Terry Kerr, by name. Curly hair, always smilin'. Trouble is, he can't walk so good, or feed himself proper. 'Spastic' disease, or somethin' like that they say. Poor kid. An' I hear it costs plenty to keep him in a place where he can get proper attention and a lot of treatment that just might help him. You know who I mean.'

Wade came up off the ground with a mighty effort and swung a fist hard under Frank's jaw. Greer floundered back at least six feet before falling awkwardly in a tangle of arms and legs, mouth bloody, eyes glazed.

Tex Lyle and Bugs Tyrell closed swiftly on the still groggy Wade. Lyle gun-whipped him to his knees, but then Frank spat some blood, held up a hand.

'Leave him be. He's just givin' me the sign that he's gonna help us out. Ain't that so, Yancey? Sort of a 'no choice' offer, huh?'

The grey eyes looked as if they could spit .45-calibre bullets. But Frank's crooked smile stayed put.

He knew blamed well he had made his point.

5

Found

'By all that's holy! It's *him*!'

Mattie Groom looked up sharply from rolling out dough for a piecrust in the large kitchen section of the new way station; the Mexican cook was stirring a stew nearby.

Behind Mattie, at a small table where he was having a cup of coffee with his bacon, eggs and beans, Walt Dedman stood quickly, knocking over the straight-back chair he had been sitting on. He ignored it, stared down intently at the folded newspaper he held and which had arrived with supplies from Eton's Creek barely an hour earlier.

He turned towards the staring girl; she was brushing a strand or two of her chestnut hair back from her forehead, floury hand leaving a small smear across her bronzed skin. Dedman tapped the newspaper, a Fresno publication: the *Sundowner Gazette*, and strode across to her work table.

'Look! That's him, isn't it?'

'Who?' she asked before looking more closely at the paper, then seeing an artist's black-and-white impression of a male head and shoulders, his battered hat pushed back off his brow. His face had a lot of marks on it that might have been meant to represent cuts or bruises. 'Who is it?'

He made an exasperated sound and moved closer, thrusting the paper towards her. 'Look, woman! You must recognize him. The artist has done a very good likeness, even down to the lighter shading of those eyes.'

Mattie gave a small gasp, put a hand to her mouth briefly. 'Well, I'm not sure. I only glimpsed him in lamplight, and that from several feet away, but it *looks* like the man who brought you in to the ranch.'

'It *is*!' He slapped the paper again

over the picture. 'Wade! That's the name they give him here.' He suddenly dropped into a chair, holding the paper in his left hand and absently massaging his shoulder, moving his neck as well to ease some of the pain spasms that were the legacy of the bullet in his back. His lips moved a little as he hurriedly read the accompanying text. There was a half-smile on his face as he looked at Mattie. 'He's a hero again, too.'

Mattie frowned a little. 'Not one of those 'professional' heroes who go around setting everything to rights?'

Dedman frowned, annoyed. 'Nothing of the sort. It says here he was riding shotgun on the McFadden-to-Lacey stage when there was an attempted hold-up. The stage crashed, badly injuring the driver; later he had a leg amputated because of his injuries. But this Wade shot and killed one of the robbers, someone called Dexter, although pretty badly injured himself. It apparently scared the others off, though.'

He turned the paper this way and

61

that, taking it closer to the window for better light.

'Mmmmm. I think the artist has tried to include some of his wounds, but it makes him look like he's been in a brawl — or taken a beating of some kind. Which, I suppose, he has, if he was thrown from the stage. Anyway, he did what he could for the driver and passengers, who have nothing but praise for him, then he started to *walk* through that atrocious boulder-strewn country, until he happened across a band of mustangers.'

He paused as he looked for something in the text. 'Ah, yes, here it is: *Four or five men, led by someone named Frank Greer . . . They returned with him to the stage and . . .* ' He folded the paper over. 'Well, never mind the details, but they jury-rigged the coach somehow, strengthening splintered wheelspokes with green saplings, hitched up the surviving team horses and eventually got everyone safely to Lacey. Guess they all deserve high praise.'

He shook his head admiringly. 'But that man Wade's a natural-born hero, Mattie. And now I know where to find him.' He started for the door. 'I don't know when I'll be back but I'm going to town to get some telegrams away to Lacey. I hope I'm in time to catch Wade — *and* his friends.'

Mattie blinked. 'You're bringing him here?'

'Of course. I've waited all this time to find him and now I'll have a chance at last to repay him the way he deserves.'

Mattie hesitated, then smiled slowly as she returned to her piecrust-making. 'I think I'd better have Conchita help me make two or three apple pies.'

'Good idea. We'll make it a celebration. I'll bring something appropriate from town for the toast. Oh — and invite Jason. I wouldn't want his nose any further out of joint than he already thinks it is. Pity, that.'

Mattie looked at him, suddenly sober. 'You're a good man, Walt. It does bother me the way Jason reacted when you gave me the catering concession for the stageline. I — I really thought letting him run the ranch would please him, but he seems quite surly. As if he's been . . . *put* upon.'

'Well, he's young. What, barely twenty? Probably just scared off by the sudden responsibility. I'll make sure he knows there's always help here if he wants it.'

She smiled again then. 'Like I said: a *good* man.'

★   ★   ★

Wade was not happy with all the publicity Frank Greer had deliberately generated after the phoney 'rescue' of the stage. No, not so much 'phoney', but the stage's rescue had been 'staged' by the man who had fully intended to rob it and likely shoot up the passengers into the bargain. Had to be some sort of irony in that, even if it didn't work out the way Frank had originally planned.

Wade had no choice but to go along with what Frank wanted. That miserable son of a bitch had tied his hands well and truly the moment he brought young Terry Kerr into the deal. His gut twisted and knotted at the thought: the urge to kill Frank was so strong he could barely keep his food down. How the hell did he know about the boy?

But Frank held all the aces and he knew it; it amounted to simple, cold-blooded blackmail: play along, or the kid would die.

Frank Greer had exactly the right sort of mind to take advantage of this particular situation. 'Made to order, Yancey, *amigo*. You saved Dedman's life and he's bustin' a gut to reward you. Which is perfect for what I got in mind. All we gotta do is bring you two together and we're on our way to makin' a mighty big killin'. Frank had paused and winked. '*Actual* killin', if necessary, but I . . . Hey, come on! Look a bit enthusiastic! We're all gonna be rich!'

Wade knew *someone* would be *very* rich, and it wouldn't be him. But whatever happened, Wade had to go along with Greer. For now, leastways.

Otherwise, young Terry would be killed; he never doubted for a second that Frank would carry out his threat.

He actually cringed when he realized how long Frank must've known about Terry. According to Greer, he had it all worked out; for some time now he'd had someone, male or female, he wouldn't say, who worked in the Montville sanatorium where Terry was a patient, way up in the clear clean air of Humphrey's Peak: 13,000 feet high, though the sanatorium was only about 5,000 feet up the slopes.

This 'friend' of Greer's could reach the kid at any time. Apparently he (or she) was an experienced 'Patient Aide' as they called the attendants, sometimes giving Terry his medication which, at last news, was beginning to show some promise, bringing a mild improvement in the boy's condition — and any improvement was desirable. But if this 'friend' of Greer's received a wire from

Frank containing a certain word — which Frank did not reveal — the medication would be stopped or changed and Terry could — *would* — die.

'Simple, see?' Frank had finished, eyes narrowed and his six-gun was now held on Wade, who looked like he wanted to kill him. 'Do what I say, work with Dedman and get all the info we need about that Sundown Run with the gold, and everyone's happy — on our side, anyways. Look at it this way: you'll be rich enough to send the kid to one of them big hospitals back East, or even over to Europe, where the really smart doctors can help him.' He paused and leered. 'I know you don't even have to think about it, Yancey. You can see I'm doin' you one damn big favour, right?'

Wade admitted to himself that the part about being able to afford top treatment and care for the boy would be fine. But he knew it would never happen.

Frank had never been a man who liked sharing his *dinero*, and Wade figured he wasn't about to change.

For now, Wade had no choice: he *had* to go along with Greer and the others, whether he liked it or not.

He had to agree to the publicity in the damn newspaper so that Walt Dedman could find him and lavish on him whatever reward he had in mind — so long as it involved Wade working at the new way station when the Sundown Run came through with its cargo of refined gold bars from the very rich Fiddler's Green mine.

Wade was pretty certain Frank Greer didn't intend that he should survive the taking of that gold.

Maybe no one else would, either, apart from Frank's gang, but then, even that was uncertain.

A man who would shoot a seventy-year-old woman three times and seriously threaten the life of a six-year-old crippled boy was capable of anything.

Wade amended his thought: No — Frank Greer wasn't a man — he was a homicidal maniac.

'You must've been workin' on this for

a long time,' Wade had said quietly and Frank gave him a bleak, deadly look.

'Yeah. Ever since you hit me in the face during that Express office hold-up. That's the biggest mistake you ever made, Yancey, old pard!'

'Jesus! You really are loco, aren't you?'

Deadpan, Frank Greer said, managing somehow to look modest,

'Aw, shucks. You ain't seen nothin' yet.'

*   *   *

Frank decided to make it look good.

'Can't make it too easy for this Dedman, boys. Don't think he'd suspect anythin' much, he'll be so damn excited about finally locatin' good old Wade here. But we play it casual like, as if we din' think much about helpin' Wade get that stage and its passengers to Lacey. Like it was the kinda good deed we been doin' all our lives, because we're really nice fellas. OK?'

69

He got a couple of smiles and a chuckle. But not from Wade, who only gave him a squint-eyed glare.

'You're really enjoying this, ain't you, you bastard?' he said quietly, and Frank's grin tightened just a little as he shrugged his big shoulders and spread his arms.

'Just like to see things goin' smoothly as we can make 'em. Gotta be sure your halo ain't tarnished in any way.'

'Put it into words of one syllable, Frank, so we can all savvy what the hell you're talking about.'

Frank's smile faded and he watched, tight-mouthed, for a long, dragging minute until he eventually gave a small nod.

'Simple. We don't want Dedman thinkin' we're just a bunch of freeloaders, cuttin' ourselves in for a slice of the cake because we're Yancey's *amigos*.' His look had a challenge in it but Wade didn't react. 'So, they already think we're mustangers that Wade ran across after that stage pile-up. OK. We trap ourselves a

70

couple dozen wild broncs, break their spirit a bit so's they're manageable. Then we drive 'em to that new way station on Sundown Ridge and ask Agent Dedman, all innocent like, if he's in need of any good broncs for relay teams for his stageline. Then when he's lookin' over the hosses, he finds Good Ol' Yancey Wade with our team. And . . . ' He glared at Wade. 'I gotta spell it out any more? Or you got enough brains to see how Dedman's gonna do a backflip. He might even kiss you on both cheeks.'

Wade held Frank's stare for a long moment, then nodded once.

'So that's why we moved out of Lacey right after that rag of a newspaper hit the town. Keep Walt Dedman with his tongue hangin' out, getting all het up when he thinks he's missed catching up with me once again. Then suddenly, I show up on his doorstep. Gotta hand it to you, Frank. You might be a mean son of a bitch, but you're a smart one.'

'Did you ever doubt it?'

Frank leered at Wade and Yancey knew the man was reminding him that he'd found out about young Terry Kerr, and it was all he needed to keep Wade in line.

Thing was, Yancey Wade didn't *need* any reminding. He was living with it, night and day, ever since the boy had been mentioned.

And he *still* didn't know how Frank Greer had learned of Terry Kerr's existence.

6

Gratitude

They were lucky, finding a big bunch of wild horses led by a rolling-eyed, snorting, foot-stomping white stallion that folk had spoken about for years as the 'Ghost Stallion of Bearcat Ridge'.

In its day the stallion had stomped a couple of the locals on its forays into farm gardens, or had just gone thundering his harem through ranch yards for the sheer hell of it.

'You'll never catch that sonuver,' one small rancher told them, shaking his head. 'He's a mean bastard an' I reckon he'll sacrifice his damn harem if it means he'll escape a rope round his neck and a saddle on his back.'

'Sounds like he might've run into mustangers before,' allowed Wade.

'He has. We knows for sure he's

stomped two men to death and crippled at least one.'

'Whyn't you shoot him?' demanded Greer, tired of all this stupid talk about 'ghost' horses.

The rancher backed up a step, shaking his head emphatically. 'Whoa! There's a kinda legend hangin' around that white mankiller. No one wants to shoot him. Word is, the one who does it is hexed for the rest of his life.'

'Ah, for Chris'sake!' Frank growled, fumbling out a silver dollar and pressing it into the surprised rancher's hand. 'Here. Thanks for your help, if you can call it that. You just stay outta our way when we set up our blinds and chutes. Or you could be the one to stop a bullet, not the white stallion.'

'Hey! No need for that kinda talk! I was just . . . '

But the men were following Frank now. He led them up into the hills and within an hour they were felling saplings and brush, cutting a narrow trail through the timber that could only lead to one place: camouflaged corrals big enough to contain at least twenty horses.

★   ★   ★

It was a big job and they lost much sweat and quite a bit of hide. Clothes were ripped, boot heels snapped, hands at first calloused then blistered and, when the filmy domes broke and the stinging liquid poured out, many new epithets were invented to be added to that legendary, unwritten *Dictionary Of Cusses* every range rider knew by heart.

After a day's work the lucky ones who hadn't drawn nightwatch and were waiting for the mustangs to come over to their territory to see what was going on, or to drink at the nearby creek, stripped off and plunged and cavorted in the stream's chill waters.

Frank and the others were back at the campsite, Wes Toohey having drawn the short straw as cook for this night.

Wade was sitting on a rock on the

bank of the creek wringing out his newly washed socks. He watched as Toohey, grunting a little with his rheumatics, knelt and filled the coffee pot and a big saucepan.

'Got a minute, Wes?'

Toohey snapped his head up, glanced at Wade, bit his lower lip, then nodded and grunted again when he stood. He ambled across. 'Boys're waitin' on supper. Can't stay long.'

Wade's grey eyes held to the older man's face. 'You know what I'm goin' to ask you.'

Wes put on the worst imitation of a puzzled man that Wade had ever seen and, despite himself, he smiled and held up his hand as Toohey started to carry it through.

'Don't bother, Wes. Just answer me. When I gave you that letter to mail for me back in Carson City because Frank was all antsy about the train hold-up, did you post it?'

Wes tightened his lips, hung his head, moved it once in a negative shake. 'Like you said, Frank was all tippy-toes an' jumpy, made me check the shotguns over 'n' over. Letter fell outta my shirt pocket and he picked it up an' . . . '

'He open it?'

Toohey heaved a sigh. 'He did. Once he seen the address, that Arizona hospital at Montville . . . Look, Yancey, I'm really sorry, pard. It's — it's bothered me some. Hell! bothered me a *lot*! Frank moves his lips when he reads, an' murmurs; so I got the gist of it. Was about a boy there, an' you pay for his treatment or somethin' . . .

Wade swore. 'And Frank read all about him in my letter. Goddammit, Wes, you might've told me.'

Toohey looked up, hangdog, but with a hard glitter in his eyes now. 'I know. But I din' think anythin' of it at the time. I mean, so your kid's in hospital an' — '

'He's not my kid. And I'm not explaining, Wes. But because of that damn letter, Frank got all the informa- tion he needed to throw me over a

77

barrel!' He drove his right clenched fist into the palm of his left hand. '*Goddammit*!'

'Ah, geez, Yancey!' Wes actually squirmed. 'I — I — '

'What happened to the money that was in the envelope?'

Toohey licked his lips. 'I guess Frank kept it. He offered me twenty bucks a few days later, but I didn't take it.'

'Well, it's too late now. OK, Wes, it's not your fault. No! Don't let's get into a back-and-forth thing about how it happened. It *did* happen and Frank has me with a ring through my nose and a damn short rope attached.'

'What — what're you gonna do?'

'Whatever the sonuver wants me to do! If I don't, it all comes back on the boy, and Frank's crony who's caring for him.'

His voice trailed off and Wes Toohey murmured, 'Anythin' I can do — to make amends, kind of?'

Wade shook his head. 'Just leave it be, Wes. Just leave it be. It's my

78

problem, but I could wish like hell for a simpler one.'

★ ★ ★

They got themselves a bunch of twenty-three horses. By the time they were broken-in enough to take a bridle and saddle without chewing a man's arm off, Walt Dedman, at the way station, was practically tearing his hair.

'Dammit, Mattie!' he said for the hundredth time, pacing back and forth across the big kitchen. 'I've sent telegraph messages all over and no reply worth the paper it's written on! *Someone* must know where Wade is! He's got to know by now I'm looking for him.'

'How could he not know, the way you've spread the word?' She looked up at him as she put the lid on the coffee pot and poured two cups. 'Walt, did you ever think . . . he mightn't want to be contacted?'

Dedman frowned, stopped pacing. 'Doesn't want to face me? But he knows by now I'm not going to cause him any trouble. All I want to do is to reward him.'

'He may not want your reward — or the publicity that will go with it.'

Dedman dropped into a straightback chair as she placed the coffee cups on the table. 'You mean — he might not be in the law's good books — for want of a better way of putting it?'

'Well, look at what you know; you still think that it was a posse chasing him when you were shot in the back. He didn't want to hang around, got out of there as fast as he could — actually left you, wounded.'

'But he came back, Mattie. That's the part I remember. No matter what trouble he's in, if he's in any; he came back for me. And I wouldn't be here right now if he had just ridden away. I'd never have been able to take up this job — never have met you.'

She smiled and spoke slowly as she pushed the sugar bowl across the table. 'Well, I would be disappointed about that.' Was there a slight hesitation there?

'Now that's what I like to hear! What the devil . . . ?'

He jumped up and ran to the door, opening it swiftly as he heard the wild yells cowboys usually reserve for herding cattle. There was even the thunder of hoofs.

'My God! It's a bunch of horses and their riders — streaming into the yard, and . . . '

She was beside him now as the riders raced their mounts back and forth, except one who jumped for the rails of one of the big empty corrals, riding the long-bar gate as he swung it open. He was lost in the dust as the bunch of whinnying, snorting, thundering horses were driven in. Yelling riders seemed to be everywhere, hazing the frightened animals through the gate. The horses milled and pranced. One or two older ones reared up and pawed at the top rails. Others, senses reeling, nipped nearby companions in their sudden terror and frustration at their freedom coming so abruptly to an end.

Then two men broke away and came towards the main building where the girl and Dedman stood, squinting into the sun, now dimmed with the roiling dust cloud. Walt stiffened, leaned forward, peering hard at the newcomers.

'Isn't that . . . ?' Mattie started to say.

'By Godfrey! I believe it is. It's *him*! *Wade*! And the man beside him is the other one the newspaper interviewed.'

'Frank Greer!'

She jumped almost a foot high as Dedman let out a wild rebel yell. 'Come on up, boys! We're mighty glad to see you. And we'll make sure you'll be mighty glad you came.'

★ ★ ★

The way station's Mexican cook, under Mattie's supervision, made a fine lunch for the hungry mustangers. Walt Dedman, so pleased that at last he had Yancey Wade under the same roof as himself, broke out some of his bonded stock of rye whiskey, which went down well in more ways than one with the wild, hard-eyed men in from the desert mountains.

Wade had little to say and looked positively embarrassed when Dedman approached the subject of rewarding him for rescuing the stageline man.

'Mr Dedman — ' Wade started, but was interrupted.

'Walt, please!'

'OK, Walt. I feel I'd be taking any reward under false pretences. I — I'd fully intended to ride off — '

'Because you had no choice,' Dedman cut in again. 'Yes, I understand that now. I've given it plenty of thought. My conclusion is that *nothing* matters except the fact that you *did* come back and save my life.' He turned to Mattie in the seat beside him at the long table, and lightly placed a hand on her brown fore-arm. 'Not only that, but because of your efforts, I was able to meet this fine woman. And I'm hoping that will be another landmark in my life.'

Mattie flushed in embarrassment,

nudged him, her smile a little strained. Walt laughed and Wade raised his glass with the rye glinting like gold in it.

'Here's to you, ma'am. Reckon an invite to the wedding would be reward enough for me.'

Dedman looked at her, an unspoken appeal in his eyes, not quite so confident now. Mattie, still smiling, but a mite flustered, said, 'Let's not get too far ahead of ourselves. We have to get this way station up and running.'

There was a chorus of agreement. When the noise subsided a little Frank threw a glance in Wade's direction, spoke loudly across the table.

'Mr Dedman, sir, as you can see our friend Yancey likes to hide his light under a bushel. No, no, Yance, let me finish. You ain't dodgin' out on this issue.'

'I should say not!' said Dedman emphatically, softening the sharp tone with a smile and raising his own glass towards Wade. 'I've waited a long time for this day and no shilly-shallying is going to deny me the pleasure of offering you a job, right here on this brand-new way station: a good-paying job. What d'you say, Yancey?'

'Hey, fellers!' shouted Frank, raking his hard gaze around at his men, letting it come to rest on Wade. 'Ain't that a great offer? Yance, it's gotta be Fate! Why it's only twenty-four hours since you said to me, 'I sure wouldn't mind a wranglin' job on a place like that new way station . . . ''

Dedman snapped his head around to look at Wade. 'You actually said that?' he asked, and not waiting for an answer, went on: 'Head wrangler is just what I had in mind, Yancey. It entails a good deal of responsibility: making sure the relay teams are properly broken to harness and not going to cause any trouble for our passengers; having spares, if needed; watching schedules; keeping gear in top condition — '

'There you are, Yance!' Frank cut in again, allowing himself to sway a little as if he was beginning to feel his liquor.

'Made to order. You're a top man at all them chores.' He turned quickly to Dedman. 'Mr Dedman, sir, I hope I ain't outta order but — well I've always been a man who, when he sees a chance, a good chance, I makes a grab at it. Sir, would you consider givin' me an' the boys a contract for supplyin' the relay mounts? I mean, all of us have been workin' together for a l-o-n-g time an' we know our job an' each others' minds, you might say. I ain't a man for big words and cain't think of the right one just now, but . . . '

'You have a certain — *rapport*, perhaps?' Walt Dedman suggested, accepting his refilled glass handed to him by Wes Toohey. 'Well, I see no reason why it shouldn't be a very good deal, judging by the quality of those horses you brought in. What d'you think, Mattie, my dear?'

Mattie's smile still seemed forced to Wade. 'I'm just the supervisor for the vittles, Walt. You know best about what's needed with your men. I'm sure you'll choose carefully.'

She let it hang and Dedman blinked, aware the liquor was getting to him a little: he decided he liked the feeling. He squared his shoulders and cleared his throat.

'Can I make the toast, Mr Dedman?' Frank Greer cut in, getting to his feet, allowing a slight sway to show again. He raised his glass. 'Lady — and gennlemen: fill your glasses, an' be upstandin' and let's all drink to the — er — total success of the Sundown Stageline's new venture. May everyone, passengers and employees — oh, and employers, of course, Walt — may we all be happy — an' er *winners* — in ways bigger'n better'n we ever dreamed of!'

They drank, Wade's face carefully blank, Mattie unable to keep the frown from her tanned face, and Walt Dedman nodding full agreement, mellow and happy.

'Fine speech, Frank, fine speech,' he said, slurring a little. 'You echo my sentiments exactly.'

'Now ain't that somethin',' Frank said, tipping a wink at Wade. 'Looks like

87

we're on a winnin' streak this time, Yancey, ol' pard? Make up for some of our past losses.'

'That sounds like you knew each other before you — *stumbled* upon Mr Wade after the attempted stagecoach hold-up?' Mattie commented, looking steadily at Frank.

Greer frowned and licked his lips. 'Oh? I thought you knew. Yeah, we'd knowed each other in the army. Dodged a lotta Reb bullets together, din' we, ol' pard?'

He said the last two words with a faint emphasis, which might or might not have been detected by Mattie — and Dedman. Yancey nodded briefly. 'Seems a long time ago.'

'Well, old friends working together sounds like a good thing to me,' Walt Dedman said. 'Gents, at risk of making your heads swim, fill your glasses once again while we drink a toast to our new team. I reckon I can now officially declare this here way station open for business! Down the hatch, gents, and then let's sample the kind of good food we'll be serving our paying passengers.'

* * *

They were seated around the long table that the through-passengers would be using, making a good meal out of the crusty beefsteak pie with boiled or mashed potatoes, green peas from Mattie's ranch garden and the inevitable *frijoles* in a hot Mexican sauce that was the favourite recipe of the Spanish cook, Conchita.

It was convivial and noisy and Mattie looked up from her plate across the table at Dedman who, flushed and bright-eyed, was obviously enjoying himself in this rowdy company.

'Walt, our crew quarters aren't ready yet. In fact they've barely been started,' she pointed out quietly.

Dedman stared, then blinked a little, getting his brain into gear. 'Oh. You mean where are Frank and his men going to sleep?' He frowned. 'Yes. I — I've overlooked that, I'm afraid, but — '

'Aw, no problem, Walt,' Frank said quickly. 'We're used to sleepin' rough. Fact we're used to all kindsa ranch chores. We can camp out behind here and *build* the damn crew quarters if you want. We don't need any more hosses right away. An' we'll be earnin' our keep. How's that sound?'

Mattie started to raise a protest and she noticed how quickly Wade's head came up, but just as Dedman was about to say something, a man appeared in the doorway. All eyes turned towards him.

Mattie stood quickly, smiling as she went towards the newcomer. 'Jason! Oh, I'm so glad you decided to come. Well, step inside and Conchita'll bring you some food while you meet the new crew that Walt has just hired.'

Jason Groom was a medium-tall, well-built young man of twenty, with a smooth face that as yet would only occasionally feel the kiss of a razor. He smiled tentatively, looking around at the others as he took off his hat, revealing

90

curly chestnut hair that was a match for Mattie's.

'Howdy, gents. I'm Mattie's brother. I've been tryin' to run our ranch, such as it is, while she's makin' a new career for herself up here, with Walt.' If he noticed the warning look Mattie gave him, he ignored it. 'But I could sure use some help, if any of you fellers want a change of jobs? I mean, I got an empty bunkhouse — not all that big, but . . . '

Mattie's smile tightened as she fought the urge to frown at Jason, holding out her hand towards him. 'You're doing a fine job, Jason.' She forced a brief laugh. 'But it's not good manners to try to poach men from Walt when he's just hired them! Now, let me introduce them to you.'

Jason ignored her censure but kept his smile, turned towards Frank Greer and his men as Walt swayed to his feet again and announced: 'Pardon the interruption, Jason. Actually, I think your — er — 'poaching' may solve a small problem for us. How would you

91

like to put up these new Sundown employees in your bunkhouse? For a nominal rent, of course. Your ranch is only half a mile or so away and it'll only be until we get crew quarters of our own here. You can benefit from their knowledge and when not helping you they can come up here and work on the crew quarters.'

'Walt, that is one brilliant idea!' shouted Frank Greer. He let his gaze settle on Wade's sober face as he lurched to his feet. His grin was a mite lopsided. 'What you think, Yance? We can be right on the spot or just a frog's leap away. Huh? You figure that's a good idea?' He nodded a little for emphasis. ''Course you do! Just about perfect, ain't it, eh, *amigo?* Ab-so-lutely perfect!'

'I'll drink to that!' shouted Tex Lyle.

'Hell!' rasped Bugs Tyrell. 'We'll all drink to it!'

Walt Dedman, smiling a mite cock-eyed, hurriedly grabbed the bottle and began topping up the glasses.

He was one happy man.

7

Wade's Run

Wade, being the bronc-stomper, as Jason Groom called him, had his work cut out with the twenty-three half-broke mustangs.

None of them had settled very well into the corrals and two had been found with badly injured bellies, one with some broken ribs, where they had tried to leap over the high fence but had only succeeded in hurting themselves.

Both had to be put down and Mattie saw by Wade's face how he hated doing it. He was preparing his rig for breaking in one of the remaining horses when Frank Greer rode in.

He looked hung-over and drank deeply from the well before dismounting carefully and walking across.

'Thought you'd be helping out

Jason,' observed Wade.

Frank gave him a sour smile. 'Others can do that. Figured I better check on you, see if you needed a hand. Them roustabouts don't look as if they know much about handlin' unbroke broncs.' He squinted as Wade moved and allowed sunlight to slap across Frank's gaunted face. ''Sides, had to make sure you din' have a change of mind. I know you and your stupid codes, and I seen the way you was lookin' at Mattie.'

Wade frowned. 'You're crazy. She's practically Mrs Dedman. Now you're here, you can lend a hand. I'm about ready to start the bustin'.'

Frank held up a hand. 'Well you go ahead. I'll come back later.' He looped his reins loosely over a corral rail, straightened out his crushed hat a little and started to walk towards the main station building, steadily, but with effort.

'What the hell you doing?'

'Feelin' kinda poorly. See if good ol' Walt'll gimme a hair of the dog. Failin' that, mebbe a few cups of Conchita's java.'

'You might's well have stayed down at the ranch,' grumbled Wade. He picked up his rig and draped it over the corral's top rail.

Frank merely gave a half-wave without turning round, kept walking. Wade swore and lifted a boot to one of the lower rails and started to remove his spurs' straps.

* * *

Frank had had one snort of Walt's rye, carefully measured by Dedman, who was also hung-over but not as badly. Now, Frank sipped his third cup of Conchita's strong Mexican coffee. He was standing at a window that over-looked the corral area, watching the controlled violence as Wade rode a paint mare into submission. He turned his head as he heard footsteps behind him, nodded to Mattie.

She was looking past him at Wade

astride the paint, his right arm flinging high and wide for balance as the horse bucked and sunfished and tried to scrape his leg along the corral fence. Wade avoided the crippling move expertly and Mattie was surprised to find she had put a hand to her mouth, afraid his leg was going to be broken — as the horse intended.

'He certainly seems to know what he's doing,' she commented.

'Yancey? Sure does, ma'am. He's one of them fellers that's good at whatever he tackles.'

'He makes it look so — easy.'

'Got that knack, too.' Maybe a trace of envy there.

She frowned slightly as she looked at Frank. She didn't like the man, for no good reason that she could name: it was just one of those occasions when there was instant dislike — and distrust. Maybe it was mutual.

'You think a lot of him, don't you?'

'Yance? Sure. We been together a lot of years.'

He was watching Wade as he spoke, not looking at Mattie. So she took him by surprise when she asked, '*Was* that a sheriff's posse that was chasing him? When they shot Walt by mistake?'

Frank looked at her slowly. 'I wouldn't know, ma'am. I wasn't there.'

'Let's put it this way: *Could* a lawman's posse have been chasing Wade — for any reason?'

'You'd have to ask him.' Frank was curt, didn't like the slant of the questions. 'I hadn't seen him for a spell.'

'Oh, I thought you — all of your men and Wade — might have been together and then split up, and he was the unlucky one who drew the posse.'

Frank held her gaze and he was pleased when he saw how uncomfortable she was at the look on his face. 'You make it sound like we're a bunch of desperadoes, on the run.'

'It had occurred to me. I mean, that was rather . . . fortuitous, you meeting up with Wade that way, when he was going for help.'

By now Frank was rolling a cigarette, hands a mite trembly, but from his hang-over (he told himself), not from Mattie's probing. 'You sayin' Yancey ain't really the hero folk take him for?'

'Oh, I don't know that I would go that far. Only that I do find it surprising that no trace was ever found of the men who attempted to hold up the stage that crashed.'

'Just one of them things.' Frank lit the cigarette with jerky motions, blew smoke deliberately towards her face, forcing her to move back.

In the corral Wade was just climbing down from the panting, sweating horse, calling to one of the roustabouts to come lend a hand: apparently the cinchstrap wasn't as tight as it should be and they could hear his raised voice — but not the actual words — as he gave the surly roustabout a tongue-lashing.

Frank could see she was distracted and spoke up, figuring to take her thoughts further away from the line she had been following.

'Yancey's a genuine hero, ma'am. Nothin' snide or sly about him. They give him a coupla medals in the army and the cap'n had to *order* him to accept one, 'cause Yance figured he hadn't earned it.'

Mattie was really interested now. 'He actually refused?'

'Aw, he had to accept it in the end, 'cause he was ordered to.' Frank shook his head, blowing his exhaled smoke away from her now that he had her attention. 'Was durin' the Battle of Crucifix Crossin' on the Missouri. Not such a big battle, that is in *fightin'* terms, but mighty important to us Yankees. We needed control of the river, see?'

'I do know about that battle. My eldest brother was killed there.'

'That so? Well, it was a God-awful place. There'd been heavy rains and floods. Nothin' but a sea of mud and our platoon was trapped with our backs to the river — and no boats to get us across. The Rebs outnumbered us seven ways to Sunday. They wanted control of that crossin', too. Anyways, when the cap'n called for volunteers to take a message upriver to where we had control of Parson's Landin', Yancey put up his hand, said he'd been there before.

'Well, it was pure hell. The Rebs wanted us dead or outta there pronto, and they was attackin' and we counter-attacked as best we could. But there was a *wall* of lead across all that mud almost every minute of the day or night. It was a mighty big Reb army we were up against.'

He paused, drew deeply on his cigarette. She could see by his eyes he was remembering that terrible time.

'No Rebs were abroad where Yancey was headed, so if somethin' moved it had to be a Yankee and the Rebs poured the lead on. Two days and nights Yancey was out there in that muddy hell, workin' and squirmin' his way a few feet at a time. Had his first bayonet fight there, too, skewered the Reb who was a boy of only about sixteen. Told me he almost gave up then. Seriously wanted outta the damn war. Anyways, he was wearing a heavy, full-length coat, 'cause it was winter and the mud and rain was freezing. When he got across and could rest up a spell, he found the bottom of that coat was shredded all to hell. Later, someone figured it must've taken at least a hundred bullets to chop it up so bad. An' Yancey's pack was shot off his back, just the straps left.'

'And — and he wasn't wounded?'

'No, ma'am. We all reckoned it was a plain miracle. He carried his musket slung across his back, the fore end slanted up behind his head. He was almost to our sentry line when the Johnnies opened up with a coupla cannon. He felt somethin' sock him in the back of his head and passed out.

'He come to, lyin' in the mud. Figured the Rebs musta left him for dead, because a piece of shrapnel had hit his rifle, taken out a big chunk of the wood from the forestock and then banged him behind the ear. Knocked him cold and he bled like a stuck hog.

'But he crawled the rest of the way, got our message through an' our boys got boats an' rafts down to us, evacuated the whole lot in one helluva night and . . . '

He stopped, dragged deep again and shrugged. 'You know what Yancey said when I went to see him in hospital? 'I'm turnin' in my bayonet, Frank. I know we have to kill Rebs, but I never want to get that close again an' look into their eyes.' Yeah. Wasn't worried about his own wound or nearly dyin' from exhaustion, feet all cut to hell, or even that he'd saved us all. Just couldn't stop thinkin' about that kid he'd had to stick with cold steel.'

Mattie winced at the image the words conjured up. She said, her voice a trifle shaky, 'It must have been an awful time for all of you.'

'Yes'm, it was. Yancey's effort went

down in the official history of the regiment as 'Wade's Run'.'

She nodded, looking at him squarely, not sure just why Frank had told her. Almost as if he had read her mind, he said,

'So you can see Yancey Wade's a man to ride the river with. Give him a job and he'll get it done, hell or high water. An' he'll get it done right, too.'

Her greenish eyes held to his face. 'It would seem so. I believe Walt has already decided that.'

Frank frowned, a little puzzled, and she added, 'You didn't really have to try to convince me, is what I'm saying.'

He tugged at one ear lobe, cigarette momentarily forgotten, jumped when it sizzled the hair that half-covered his ear. He stifled a curse with difficulty and she half-smiled.

'Aw, I just didn't want you gettin' the wrong idea about Yancey. I mean, he'll do the job he's hired for. I already told you that. He'll get this way station goin' like it should, too.'

'Yes. Well, you can relax, Frank: his job's safe.'

She didn't quite know why she said that last, but it had suddenly occurred to her that Frank Greer was giving Wade a character build-up to make sure his job was indeed, 'safe'. Or to nudge her mind away from the suspicion that Wade — and Greer himself — might have been dodging a posse when Dedman had been shot.

Uneasily, she wondered just why Wade's employment at the way station seemed to be so important to Greer.

8

Big Ears

Jason Groom didn't like his new crew.

They were too rough and ready, too arrogant, too . . . sloppy. Wes Toohey, the old one — well, fifty was 'old' to a lad of barely twenty years — was the best of the bunch. But even he didn't have much control over the others. Greer, the boss, spent most of his time up at the way station; Jason had heard the one called Bugs speaking with Tex Lyle, and several times he'd said that: 'Frank has to make sure Wade don't make any slip-ups and give the game away. He's got a funny notion about lyin' to people, you know; always has had.'

It meant little to Jason but he aimed to keep an ear cocked and see if he could find out more. At first he figured he should ride up to the way station and tell Walt or Mattie, but:

'Damn Mattie!' he told himself. 'She's bossed me around ever since Pa died and left her the ranch!'

Damn old fool! Made out that will when Mattie was the only child. Then when Jason came along unexpectedly six or seven years later, he never got around to changing it. He wasn't even sure his father *would*'ve changed it, seeing as Jason's mother had died soon after giving birth to him. He'd always felt the Old Man blamed him for that.

Now — *now*! Walt Dedman comes along, busting a gut to marry Mattie, telling her she could sell the ranch and Jason could come to work at the way station.

'Where they can *both* boss me around!' He wasn't aware he had spoken out loud and jumped when Wes Toohey said,

'Someone's always bossin' someone around, kid; way of the world. Thing is to ride easy with it. Fightin' that sorta thing only brings a load of grief.'

'Who asked you?' Jason knew he sounded petulant and he swore silently; he wanted to appear grown up to these men. He knew they weren't the 'best' kind, but they were tough and hard-living, which he secretly admired, and he figured it was about time he became more of a man, instead of a kid who let his elder sister tell him what to do all the time.

Wes shrugged, standing easy in the doorway, and Jason noticed for the first time that the man wore his gun in a manner he had always heard described as 'the gunfighter's way': bullet-belt slanting across the belly, gun butt at a level with the inside of Wes's thick wrist, holster cut away around the trigger guard, and the base tied down to his thigh with a rawhide thong.

Looking more closely, Jason saw there were three notches just visible, cut into the cedar butt. He snapped his gaze up to Toohey's face and as he opened his mouth to speak, Wes said,

'Somethin' foolish I did a long time ago down on the Border, lad. Figured I had to keep tally of the men I killed.'

'You were a gunfighter?'

'Figured I was then. Rode with a wild bunch. Seen 'em all get killed one by one by someone faster. There's *always* someone faster, kid. I dunno how, but I had enough sense to see that. Rode north and started workin' the cattle trails. That had its dangers, too. But a man didn't lose so much sleep wonderin' if someone was sneakin' up on his camp to put a bullet in his back.'

Jason swallowed, staring, looking thoughtful. 'I'm not much good with a six-gun. I can shoot a rifle pretty good, though.'

'Then stick with it. But keep your shootin' legal. Know what I mean, boy?'

'I'm not a dummy.' Jason bristled and Wes smiled faintly as he held up a hand.

'And keep a rein on that temper. It's damn fool touchiness that starts most fights, fists or guns.'

'I guess you'd know,' Jason said with a little sneer.

Wes sighed. 'Back in my Border days, kid, you'd be lyin' on the floor coughin' your life out by now, you back-answered me that way. But I don't rile easy these days. Too damn old and got too much rheumatism in my hands. Now, let's change the subject. I was wonderin' if you've got an extra blanket? Like I just told you, I got the rheumatiz and it's cold in these here mountains.'

'I — I dunno as I should give you another blanket. Mattie keeps ours separate from what she has for the bunkhouse — not that we've had many ranch hands for a while.'

Wes nodded before Jason had finished speaking and began to turn away. 'Forget it, kid. I wouldn't want to get you in Dutch with your big sister. I'll survive.'

Jason hesitated, then stepped to the door and called after Toohey as he strode back towards the bunkhouse.

'I — I'll see if there's one I could bring you.' He let the words drift away as Wes went into the bunkhouse without looking back. 'Aaah! He's only a broken-down old grubliner, anyway. Hell with him!'

Still, he really wouldn't mind hearing some of the tales Wes must be able to tell about his gunfighting days along the Border, even if he was only funning.

He hurried back into the house, went to his room and yanked a colourful Indian blanket off his bed. He started to fold it awkwardly as he hurried out again and made his way to the small bunkhouse. He had to cross the oblong of grassy lawn that Mattie insisted they must keep cut and neat. Her flower- and vegetable-gardens bordered either side, making a pleasant pattern, easy on the eyes against all the harsh landscape surrounding the spread.

He never wore spurs, so he made no sound approaching the bunkhouse. He slowed when he heard Wes Toohey talking, the words reaching him through the open window.

'Just a reminder. Be careful what you say around that kid. He's got eyes big as saucers and his ear's hanging out a mile. He's the kind could be mighty interested if he got a whiff of what's goin' on, and he'd blab. Bet my boots on it. He's surly. Mean in a piss-ant kinda way.'

'You reckon he's a danger then?' That was the one they called Bugs; Jason thought he looked the meanest of the bunch, though Frank Greer seemed to be the toughest.

Right now, he felt kind of queasy and jumpy at the way Toohey had said he could blab *if he knew what was going on*.

Well, what the hell was going on? He'd suspected something wasn't quite right, but Toohey was now answering Bugs Tyrell and Jason cocked an ear.

'I dunno. He may be dumb enough to be impressed by a gang like us. He's just a kid; been spoilt by his sister and resents her movin' out. He liked them old notches in my gun butt. He'd've curled up at my feet like a good ol' cur-dog if I'd told him how I got 'em.'

'Hell, wouldn't worry none about him, then,' opined the third man, Tex Lyle. 'He's actin' just like a brat who dunno much outside his own little world. Somethin' that smells of what he sees as adventure and his tongue's hangin' out around his belly-button.'

'Just be careful what you say,' said Toohey slowly and emphatically. 'This is the biggest job we've pulled or are ever likely to. Don't take *any* chances: Frank'll back me up. It ain't worth the risk, so don't go roustin' the kid just for the hell of it. I reckon he don't got much of a sense of humour, and that means trouble in the makin'.'

'Yeah, OK, Wes. You got a point, but you're older'n us and you're lookin' on this as your last chance.'

'Could well be — for any of us,' Wes admitted quietly. 'Bugs?'

'Yeah, Wes. Best play it safe, I reckon.

Frank'll bring back the times and schedules for the stage when Wade gets 'em an' you can bet *he* won't talk outta turn.'

'Right. Now, how about a hand of cards till Frank gets back?'

'Ain't we s'posed to be loadin' tools and lumber into that buckboard outside an' takin' 'em up to the way station for the crew's quarters?'

'Yeah, I b'lieve that's what we're s'posed to be doin',' agreed Toohey. 'But if Frank can take time off, I reckon we're entitled, too.'

He stopped speaking abruptly and lunged for the window — as fast as his rheumatics would allow him to, anyway.

'What the . . . ?' exclaimed Tex.

'The boy. Just hurryin' back towards the house, carryin' a blanket I asked for. Wonder if he was bringin' it down here and heard us through the window? Now he's lightin' out back to the house in one helluva hurry.'

'Judas priest!' breathed Tex Lyle, rounding on Bugs. 'And you talkin' about schedules and stuff!'

'Just watch him mighty close,' Wes said heavily. 'He's tryin to be more growed up than he is. He could show off by lettin' slip somethin' he thinks he knows.'

'Christ! Ain't we got enough worries without wet-nursin' a damn kid, too?'

Toohey looked bleakly at Bugs. 'When we don't watch what he's about, *then*'s when we got real worries.'

'Well, I'll tell you,' Tex Lyle drawled, face hard-set. 'That kid gets between me an' my retirement money, he ain't never gonna grow any older.'

Bugs nodded grimly. Toohey heaved a sigh.

'Just be careful what you say!' he said wearily. 'How many more times've I gotta tell you? *Christ!* Don't go startin' any trouble we don't need.'

'Well, if I think he's gonna be a real danger, I aim to do somethin' about it, pronto,' Tex avowed.

'Like what?' Bugs sneered. 'Cut him in for a share?'

Tex jumped to his feet, right hand dropping to his gun butt. Bugs's face went white and Wes Toohey suddenly had his six-gun in his hand, causing the others to freeze.

'You damn fool daisies! Look at you! It's just a possibility. An' we can take care of it with one hand while we roll a cigarette with the other. And here you two are sweatin' blood.' He shook his head. 'Frank was here he'd gunwhip you both right out from under your hats.'

Both men muttered unintelligible replies.

'You want to make the kid really suspicious, you're goin' about it the right way. Just watch your mouths, for Chris'sake! You find that too hard to handle, I'll personally straighten you out, so's you'll lie in your coffin nice and cosy. So leave it right there. OK?'

Their faces slowly eased into softer lines and hands dropped away from gun butts. Bugs nodded first, then Tex made a token up-down movement of his head. Wes holstered his gun and glanced out through the window.

'Kid's bringin' the blanket back. Gonna make it look like it's his first visit down here. Go along with it, make him feel at ease. If he heard anythin' he shouldn't've he'll give himself away.'

'Then what?' Bugs demanded.

'Then we'll see.'

Jason came bustling in, looking at each of them swiftly, smiling, but it wasn't an easy smile: he had to work at it. He held out the Indian blanket.

'Found this for you, Wes.'

Toohey took it and rubbed the teased wool. 'Feels good. Be nice and warm, Thanks, kid.'

'Er . . . sorry I took so long.'

Wes arched his eyebrows. 'Oh? Never noticed. We were just exercisin' our gums a little. Was no real hurry.'

Jason shuffled awkwardly. 'D'you mind not callin' me 'kid'?'

'We'll call you whatever you want,' Wes agreed easily.

'But that's what you are: a kid,' Bugs

said, not looking at Toohey.

Jason flushed. 'Everyone thinks so, thanks to Mattie. But I'm old enough to leave here to run this chicken-shit spread while she moves in with Dedman!'

'Oughtn't talk about your sister that way,' Toohey said curtly. 'She raised you, didn't she? You owe her more respect than that.'

Jason's mouth thinned and he glared at the trio. 'An' you three're s'posed to show me more respect. You're s'posed to lend me a hand with the spread, not sit around beatin' your gums.'

Bugs, Tex and Wes exchanged a quick glance, Toohey said: 'What would you like us to do, Jace?'

'Well, I need to move some of my cows to different graze. I could use a hand to do that. One of you could help me, while the others load the buckboard with whatever Greer wants for the crew's quarters up on the mountain.'

The trio were briefly silent, then

Toohey said, heavily, 'How'd you know about that? You'd left the way station to come back here before your sister suggested we could use some of the spare lumber from down here.'

Jason frowned, licked his lips. 'Aw, she asked me if it'd be all right to do that just before I left up there.'

Toohey smiled thinly, shook his head slowly. 'You'd been long gone before the subject came up, kid.'

'I asked you not to call me that!' Jason bristled and Toohey's smile widened, thinned out.

'Well, that could divert us off the subject if we got into a discussion about whether you're a kid or not, so we'll just forget it. Tex, you don't mind helpin' the — er — Jace here to move his cows, do you? Bugs an' me'll take that load of lumber and tools up the mountain.'

Tex nodded, staring hard at Jason, who suddenly turned and left, saying, 'Suit yourselves. Just as long as someone gives me a hand.'

They watched him stomp back across the oblong of lawn and Bugs said quietly, 'He heard us talkin' all right. Musta got spooked and went back to the house, then tried to fool us with the second comin'. We got us trouble, Wes.'

'Well, we're watchin' for it now. No need for Frank to be told.'

He flicked his gaze from Bugs to Tex and both nodded slowly.

Frank wouldn't take kindly to the news that Jason Groom might have picked up on the real reason they were at the way station . . .

9

No Badge

It was an unscheduled stage. It came rattling down the steep trail that led to the creek crossing, then laboured up-slope towards the way station buildings.

Down at the corrals Wade was drenched in sweat and aching from scalp to toenails after almost a half-hour of buck-jumping, belly-jarring, neck-snapping violence riding the sweating paint across the corrals. The horse was now staring at him with still-mean eyes. Wade coiled his short rope. He frowned, shading his eyes as he watched the stage roll up towards the stopping-area.

'Now what the hell?' he growled aloud. He tossed the rope over the top rail of the corral and snatched at the rag of towel hanging over a nearby post. He mopped at his face as he hurried up towards the stage, feeling anger rising.

No one had told him to expect a stage this early. He didn't have a team ready and he was damned if he felt like going through all the motions of putting one together to replace the six sweat-sheened horses between the shafts of the new arrival. He recognized the driver.

'Where the hell'd you come from, Mitch?' Wade asked, a mite breathless. 'No one told me to expect you.'

'Not needin' a relay, Yancey. Just been diverted from the Long Creek run.' Mitch Danner, bewhiskered, still hauling on the traces, gestured over his shoulder. 'Special passenger for you. Throwed his weight around some; throwed my schedule out to hell an' gone, too. Just to get here.'

'I have my reasons, Mitch,' said a big, broad-shouldered man who stepped down from the passenger section. His long dark hair brushed his shoulders and his hat was flat-brimmed with a woven Indian band. He looked to be in his late forties.

From what Wade could see of his face it had sideburns and a healthy-looking frontier moustache. The passenger turned to look at Wade, who was still approaching; he stiffened and nodded.

'Wasn't expectin' to see you here, Yancey. You're a long way from home. Lost some weight, too. No doubt from all that hard-ridin', dodgin' law, eh?'

Wade paused, taking a closer look at the big man now. He felt a knotting of his belly.

'Cameron? Hell, you've sure got a bigger waistline than I recall.' It was weak, but he simply didn't know what to say, seeing a top US marshal right here and now.

'I'm retired now.' The big man walked across as two roustabouts appeared and looked lost when Mitch told them he'd be pushing on shortly and didn't need a change of teams. Cameron's frock-coat flipped open and big teeth flashed under the moustache. 'See? No badge.'

The knot in Wade's belly eased a little

122

— but only a little. He'd never heard of a federal marshal who really retired. 'What brings you up this way?' he asked cautiously.

Cameron came across with the old familiar rolling walk and Wade noticed that though the man might indeed be retired, he still wore his six-gun where he could get at it in a hurry if need be.

'Workin' for Fiddler's Green now. A prairie fire wiped out the gear wagons of the Western Union team that're bringin' in the telegraph line to here. Head Office should've had reports from Walt Dedman by now, so they sent me down to see how things are progressing.' He squinted a little. 'Heard Walt'd hired himself a crew, but I didn't know you were one of 'em.' After a slight hesitation he held out his large right hand. 'Long time no see.'

Wade took the hand tentatively, watching the blue eyes; they were just as hard and cold as he remembered them: like mountain-stream ice.

'We were never at real loggerheads,

you an' me, Yancey.'

'Could've fooled me,' Wade said. The two men gripped firmly but quickly as if each wanted his gunhand free as soon as possible. But Wade wasn't wearing his gun: it hung in its holster on the bullet-belt down at the corrals.

'You must feel at ease in your new job.' Cameron nodded his head towards Wade's gunless waist, then he smiled slowly. 'Relax. You oughta know I don't have any warrants to serve on you now.'

Wade thought of asking *why* he ought to know such a thing, but said nothing. The roustabouts were taking the chance to have a smoke, leaning against the log wall of the station. Then Mattie and Walt Dedman came out, both looking slightly puzzled.

Cameron shook Walt's hand, acknowledged the introduction to Mattie. 'Heard you had a new crew working for you, Walt. Company needed a progress report on how things're goin' here, asked me to check 'em out, seeing as the telegraph line's been delayed getting here.'

He kept his cool gaze on Yancey as he spoke, puzzling both Mattie and Walt.

They looked at the silent Wade, but he remained silent, didn't aim to say anything until he knew more about why Cameron was really here. He couldn't quite swallow that 'Good to see you for old times' sake.'

Frank Greer came slowly round the corner of the building, a hammer in his left hand, his right hanging loose, close to his holstered six-gun.

'Thought I recognized that voice, and here you are: Marshal Josh Cameron, I'll be damned.'

'You've been damned a long time, Frank, and it's ex-marshal. Just telling Yancey I'm retired.' He sobered then and added, with bitterness: 'Got a slug restin' mighty close to my ticker. Don't allow for the kinda life I used to lead. Have to take things easy now. So they kicked me out, settled me with a miserable pension. Wouldn't plump up a coop of chickens fit for the table.'

Frank smiled. 'Well, that's good

news.' He added quickly, 'That you're still alive, I mean.'

'I'm sure that's what you meant, Frank,' Cameron said sourly. He looked levelly at Dedman. 'You know you've got a couple of hardcases on your payroll, Walt?'

Dedman looked carefully from Wade to Greer. 'I believe they've had some colourful pasts, but I've had no trouble. I go by a man's deeds, not hearsay, Mr Cameron.'

'Best way. But you'll need to watch these two.'

'The hell does that mean?' Dedman was puzzled and Mattie frowned as she held on to his arm.

'Aw, mebbe I'm off target. But as you're contracted to Fiddler's Green, figure you ought to know these men have tangled with the law more'n once.'

'I have confidence in them both,' Walt said tersely.

'Uh-huh. Marshals' Service can't use me but private business can.' Cameron produced a wallet, took out a small card and handed it to Walt Dedman. 'Like it says there, I'm in charge of security for Fiddler's Green Mining Company. That covers our gold shipments, which'll be coming through here from time to time.' He looked around at the buildings and signs of ongoing work. 'Sent me down for a progress report, as you hadn't sent any. Seems you're doin' pretty well.'

Mattie frowned. 'Just what are you looking for?'

'My job is to check out the route for Sundown Stagelines, and make sure all is ready and safe for our scheduled Sundown runs and any others that might be carrying enough in the strongbox to make it worthwhile for some fool to attempt a hold-up.'

Mattie looked quickly at Wade. 'But Mr Wade has a good reputation. Walt checked.'

Dedman nodded. 'Forgive me, Yancey, but it was necessary. Despite all my . . . yearning to reward you, I had a responsibility to Sundown Stagelines. You saved my life, but I had a detective agency check on you. I know you've had some difficulties in your past, but nothing that I thought serious enough to warrant not rewarding you the way I intended. Mr Cameron? D'you have something to add?'

The big ex-marshal looked directly at Wade, who kept his face as unreadable as possible.

'Yancey was wanted, dead or alive, in Arizona a while back.' His words brought Dedman and Mattie up to their toes. 'He shot and killed a lawman, who, for reasons not relevant at the moment, tried to frame Wade for a major crime. I was finally convinced that Wade had been speaking gospel all along when he claimed that the so-called lawman was corrupt. Yancey had stumbled on proof but had to defend himself, and his shot killed the sheriff. He was immediately marked down as a fugitive with a mandatory dead-or-alive bounty.' He turned to the rigid Wade. 'I guess we hounded the hell out of you, Yancey, but you can't blame us. Once we had proof of that sheriff's guilt, though, the charges were dropped. I told your pard, Greer there, to pass you the good word.'

Wade stiffened. 'You told Frank?'

'Yes. We were holding him on a suspected-robbery charge, but a lady of not altogether high repute, shall we say, gave him an alibi that cleared him.' He broke off suddenly, frowning as he looked at Greer. 'You were damn lucky, Frank.'

Going by the expression on his chiselled face, Yancey was ready to kill Frank Greer, who merely shrugged.

'What the *hell*!' Cameron breathed, his big head swivelling from one man to the other. 'By God! Don't tell me Frank never told you?'

'He did not,' gritted Wade, his fists clenched now. He started forward but Cameron's big right fist came up, holding his six-gun.

'Easy, man. This is no place for settling grudges.' He swung towards Greer who didn't look very perturbed. 'You're even more miserable than I reckoned, Frank.'

Greer spread his hands, looking over Cameron's beefy shoulder to Wade. 'Yance, you know we ain't seen each other in over a year. How could I pass Cameron's message along?'

'We've been together for weeks. You gonna tell me you just plumb forgot?'

Greer slowly shook his head, lips pursed. 'No-o-o. I just din' *think* about it, I guess. I mean, we had a lot of catchin'-up to do an' we were on the move all the time. You wanted a steady job; so did I. I'm sorry, pard. I'll try to make it up to you.'

'How?'

Greer shrugged. 'I dunno. I mean, now you can go back to Arizona any time and not have any worries. Say! Didn't you have some kin over there was mighty poorly, in some kinda hospital? But you couldn't visit because of that dead-or-alive thing. Well, now you can. Just about any time you want.' His eyes carried his real message quite plainly: a reminder about Terry. 'Just about.'

Wade was trembling, his hands clenched so tightly that they were white. But he made no move towards Frank. The others watched, waiting for something to give.

'Yeah. It would be good to be able to go visit young Terry again.' Wade shifted his eyes to Cameron. 'Frank had some warrants out on him, too, didn't he?'

'Nothing federal that we knew of, and thanks to that whore — pardon — that *lady* who gave him an alibi. As far as I know there's no real bad crime we can *prove* agin him. 'Suspect' may be different, but . . . ' Cameron looked as if he would add to that, staring hard at Frank.

Walt Dedman said, 'Well, thank heaven for that. I don't believe in driving a man into the ground because he may've made a mistake, even a couple of mistakes, then makes a genuine effort to set things to rights.'

'Well, I'm sure tryin', Walt,' cut in Frank trying to look sincere. 'I admit I've gone off the rails a little. I mean, plenty of fellers found it hard to settle

131

down after the war and kicked over the traces. But Yancey an' me, we never did nothin' real bad an' we went and tried to live decent lives. Even squared away with a little jail time.'

'Well, you ain't changed much after all, Frank,' Cameron said suddenly, face stiff. 'You're just as fork-tongued as always.'

Greer tensed and his right hand jerked a little towards his gun, but he froze the movement and tried to look contrite.

'You were always a hard man, Cameron, *damned* hard. Can't you give a man a break? Walt here offered me this job and I figured it was a good chance to try an' kick my past. I know Yancey felt the same way.'

Wade glared but Frank smiled. 'Walt's give us both a chance, Yancey. I guess I shoulda mentioned earlier you were free to go back to Arizona, but — well, gimme a break, pard. I had myself to think of as well as the boys here. I got carried away, decided to wait a spell, an' — '

'Leave it right there, Frank. What's done's, done.'

Cameron tugged lightly at one end of his drooping moustache — the left one — leaving his right hand free.

'Walt, it's up to you whether you keep these fellers on your payroll. I shouldn't advise one way or t'other. If I could, I might say give 'em a chance, because nothin' really bad's been proved agin 'em — which don't mean they're angels, of course. But, like I say, the decision's got to be yours. You know you won't be hooked up to the Western Union telegraph line for a while yet?'

'Well, I wondered why they were behind schedule, but I'd plenty here to keep me occupied.'

'Yeah. A prairie fire wiped out their supply wagons, destroyed all the line insulators. If they'd been on schedule and you were connected, you coulda gimme what I wanted to know over the wire instead of me havin' to come all this way to find out for myself.'

Walt frowned. 'I have all my reports

ready. In fact, they're set to go. You can take them back with you.'

He broke off as Cameron, face set like a sculpture in granite, held up one big hand, shaking his head.

'I'm not the goddamn Pony Express. I came down here to make sure you had this place ready. Now what you do is send a man — or go yourself — to check with the Western Union line foreman. They have a telegraphist with them for testing the wires after they're strung. You have him wire your reports through to head office. Foreman might even be able to bring you up to date on whatever's happening with the Sundown Run. Just a suggestion. But I ain't a damn message-boy. For no one.'

It was obvious the ex-marshal was a mite touchy and felt that all this running around on his part was beneath his dignity. So Walt swallowed the tart remarks he had been about to spit out and nodded tersely.

'Sounds like a good idea. Guess I should've thought of it myself. I'm a qualified telegraphist, too, you know.'

'Yeah. Well, it's your job to see things run to schedule, and to notify head office. I'll just take a look around, see everything's up to standard.' Cameron paused briefly, nodded curtly to Wade and Frank Greer. 'You boys've got a chance now to square away a few things. Show some sense an' make the most of it.'

He strolled off towards the rear of the way station building, taking a small notebook and pencil from his shirt pocket.

No one said anything while he made his inspection. When he came back, closing the notebook and returning it to his pocket, all Cameron said was, 'Guess she'll do.'

It sounded grudging to Mattie and she tightened her grip on Walt's arm. He made no response to it, just watched Cameron closely as he strode back to the stage and the impatient driver, and clambered into the passenger section.

There was no wave as Danner, with

a string of imaginative curses, hauled the team around and brought it on to the trail leading away from the way station.

'There goes a man not real happy in his job,' observed Wade.

'Something of a come-down for someone of his reputation,' agreed Walt, turning to Yancey and Frank. 'The detective agency I hired to check on you both made a very thorough report. I know you served some time on the Yuma rockpile, Frank, and you Yancey, you did a short spell for gunning a man down in Tombstone, I believe.'

'Bull McCall. He deserved killin'. It was fair and square. Thing was, his uncle was sheriff of that county.'

Dedman nodded. 'Yes. I made the connection before I reached the end of the report. But a little more digging and I learned you also had been part of the famous — or infamous — 'Bloody Bill' Catlow Raiders during the war. A bunch with a bloodthirsty reputation.' He sighed. 'But I gave you both the benefit of the doubt, influenced by the fact that Yancey had saved my life, I guess, but I really *wanted* to reward him. So I may've skimmed across some parts of the agency's report, but I hasten to add that that was mainly because there was a lack of positive identification, no one could be definite about most of the crimes you were accused of.'

'Like what, Walt?' Mattie asked suddenly, a mite stiffly. 'I didn't know about all of this.'

'No, my dear, but I would've told you in good time.' Dedman looked at her steadily. 'It's the way I operate, Mattie. I'm prepared to give people a good length of rope. I was given very few chances myself over the years, but, in the end one decent man did offer me a break and — well, I've never looked back.' He seemed a little embarrassed as he added, 'So I figured it my duty to follow my instincts and — well, sort of pay back something whenever the opportunity occured.'

Mattie smiled slowly and pressed his arm. 'Walt, you are a man to ride the river with: I believe that's the way the Texans put it! I'm quite ready and willing to go along with whatever decisions you make.' She glanced across to Frank and Wade, both men impassive, very still, their futures now hanging on Dedman's response.

He didn't keep them waiting. 'I've already hired you and I consider I've played fair. I don't think it's too much to expect you to do the same.' His gaze flicked from one man to the other. 'D'you consider that reasonable, boys?'

'More than fair, Walt,' Wade said, meaning it.

'You got my word we won't let you down, Walt,' added Frank quickly, avoiding the sharp look Wade shot him.

'Good. Because, in case you're thinking I'm naïve or perhaps a little soft, I tell you now, that if I'm wrong, and you do let me down, then I will dedicate all of my resources to bringing you to heel; and you may be surprised at just how stubborn and ruthless I can be when I get my dander up. I have a reputation for never giving up.'

The taut silence was broken only by the buzz of insects or the occasional snort and stomp of one of the horses.

Walt's warning was only spoken words, but they landed on that sunlit ridge with the impact of an avalanche.

10

No Quarter

'You see now why I insisted we wear bandannas over our faces when we pulled a job?' said Frank somewhat smugly. 'They never proved nothin' that could stick, because no one could identify us for sure, which is just as well for us right now.'

Wade lit the cigarette he had just rolled, shook out the match as he exhaled smoke, and looked at Frank with his hard, clear grey eyes.

'You're goin' ahead with the plan to rob the Sundown Run?'

'Stupid question! Judas priest, you think I'm gonna be scared off by someone like Cameron? Hell, you heard him: he don't hold no legal clout now. He's just a workin' stiff. Older an' slower.'

'There was nothing slow about the way he got his gun out,' Wade pointed out curtly.

'Yeah, yeah. Years of practice, but he *knew* he was gonna draw. His reflexes in a tight deal won't be so good.'

'When Cameron thinks about things, he just might change his mind, and tell Walt to fire us all.'

'Be too late. Walt's got us workin' for him, his way, and he won't want to change now. Hell, he's still thinkin' mostly that you saved his neck. An' I dare say he spends more'n a few minutes each day thinkin' about Mattie, too. He'll let things stand.'

Wade's face was unrelenting. 'Walt's a decent man, Frank, like Mattie pointed out. We ain't met many of them since we left the army, or even while we was in it.'

Frank straightened; they were in the shade of a tree whose spreading branches filtered dappled shade around the area. Wes Toohey and the others had unloaded the lumber for the additions to the crew

141

quarters, and were now taking a break under another tree, looking across at Frank and Wade. They had all recognized Josh Cameron and knew his reputation.

'He's OK,' Frank said grudgingly, eyes narrowed. 'But you sound like a man who's thinkin' of mebbe droppin' out,' he added thickly.

'Thinking about it,' Wade admitted, meeting the other's hostile gaze. 'Cameron's no fool. Nor is Walt.'

'Hell, you were eager enough to join us when you figured your share would let you get a top doctor for that kid.' A not-so-subtle reminder for Wade.

'That's the only reason I've stuck so long with you, Frank. Getting the money he needs for treatment at gunpoint seemed the quickest way, even if it was the riskiest. But I was willing to chance it.'

'Hell, you'll have more *dinero* than you'll ever need, if we pull off this deal.'

Wade hesitated. 'Yeah, I'm tempted, Frank. But I've had a bellyful of you and I think that if I stick around much longer, we're gonna go head to head.'

Frank straightened, the smouldering cigarette halfway lifted towards his mouth. He stared back for a long minute, then said, 'Well, don't expect me to back down.'

'Hell, I wouldn't want you to.'

Frank's frown deepened. 'It's mostly because I never told you they'd dropped that warrant in Arizona, ain't it?'

'Partly. Also because you're such a miserable, self-seekin' son of a bitch, and I dunno why the hell I haven't beat your head in long ago.'

Frank dropped the cigarette this time, eyes slitting. 'By Christ! You're pushin' it.'

'I mean to get some things settled. This way!'

Wade swung a roundhouse right that took Frank Greer on the side of the jaw and sent him staggering out from under the tree, stumbling and flailing his arms wildly for balance, like a drunk. His antics brought Wes Toohey and the others running across just as Frank went down, rolling in the dust.

'Jesus! What's up?' demanded Bugs Tyrell, grabbing Frank's arm and starting to haul him to his feet.

Frank spat some blood, wrenched himself free of Bugs and lowered his head, charging back with a growling roar to where Wade waited, boots planted firmly, fists knotted and poised in front of his chest in the time-honored pose of a man ready to defend himself — or to deliver a bloody thrashing to his opponent.

Wade stepped forward to meet the furious Greer's charge, eager for combat. No quarter asked, none given.

Then Frank reached for his gun.

'No guns!'

Greer blinked, surprised at the roaring voice behind him. It was Wes Toohey, and he held a cocked Colt in his hand as he came up to Frank on the right-hand side. 'It don't warrant gunplay, Frank.'

'Who the hell asked you?' Frank's hand continued on its move towards his Colt; then his crushed hat spun from his head and once more he went into his drunken saraband as he tried to keep his balance. When he had managed it, Wes held Frank's gun in his left hand.

Greer started cussing but made no move towards Wes, who jerked his own six-gun in Wade's direction. 'There's the man you want to hit.'

'I'll get to you later!' Frank gritted, and suddenly rounded on Wade as the man stepped forward, just as eager as Toohey to keep this at a fists-only level — for now.

He had no doubt that later — some time — Frank would get his wish and turn the face-off into gunplay.

Then Wade had to dodge as Frank swung; he wasn't quite quick enough. Frank had a lot of power, fuelled by hatred, behind that blow, and though it only glanced off Wade's jaw, it set him stumbling and he fell to one knee.

Greer leapt in, bringing up his knee into Wade's face. Yancey wrenched his head aside but the blow still caught him on the temple and he stretched out in the dust. Frank jumped forward, lifting a boot above Yancey's head. Wade twisted, caught the descending boot in both hands and wrenched it with a breath-busting grunt.

Suddenly Frank Greer was half-flying, body almost S-shaped as he struggled to keep his balance. But his feet tangled and he fell with a thump. There was something blurred between him and the bright sun: too late he realized that it was Wade launching himself bodily. Greer started to lift his hands in an effort to ward off the crushing weight, but Wade hit like a runaway wagon and flattened him to the ground.

Inside Frank's head rang with the shouting of the onlookers, his own trio as well as Jason and a couple of roust-abouts. And just before he wrenched his head away from a whistling hammer blow, he thought he saw Walt Dedman running up, Mattie close behind.

By that time stars were exploding behind Frank's eyes and a hand with iron fingers clawed at his throat as Wade

146

straddled him. Frank grabbed with both hands but couldn't unlock the grip as he was hauled halfway up, choking as Wade's free hand hammered him between the eyes.

His ears felt as if they would explode with the pressure generated inside his skull from the impact: it made his brain reel. But the old instincts were working and he spat a mouthful of blood-tinged spittle into Wade's face.

Yancey instinctively snapped his head aside, wiping his features. Frank convulsed and brought up a knee into Wade's belly. As he was doubled up, Frank jerked his upper body violently. His bony forehead smashed across Wade's nose and blood spurted as he fell to one side. Panting, air wheezing at last into his tortured lungs, Greer got his balance, swayed a little, face blood-streaked.

Wade, blood smearing his chin, rose groggily, lurched away from the round-house right that just flicked his ear. Then Frank was all over him, crowding him back with his body weight, fists hammering, arms blurred as he pummelled and jabbed, head thrusting against Wade's chest.

Back-pedalling, his own fists and forearms parrying the solid blows, Wade felt his boots hit something uneven that made him stagger. He started to fall, putting down his left hand in an effort to steady himself. He felt some of the lumber Toohey and the others had brought for the crew quarters and had unloaded here in untidy piles.

Hell! They must've fought the entire length of the whole damn yard to end up on this random stack.

Then he crashed down as he lost footing and felt the edges of hardwood planking maul his ribs. He fell half on his face, looked up in time to see that Frank had grabbed a length of four-by-two and was swinging at his head.

He really needed more breath, but he managed to heave himself over the small stack of planks that had hurt him. There was a solid *thunking* sound an inch from his ear and Greer staggered forward with the effort of his blow.

Wade launched himself bodily, drove his head into Frank's midriff and locked his arms about the thick waist at the same time. They both went down, elbows jerking at ribcages and bloody faces, rolling through the dust. Greer had lost his grip on the length of wood but he clawed up a handful of gravel and threw it into Wade's face.

Yancey wrenched aside, half-blinded, spun back instinctively and swung his left leg in a wide arc. It caught Frank on the knee and the man yelled as his leg collapsed under him. He was quickly stretched out by one of Wade's boots to the side of his head. Wade staggered from the effort of the kick and was surprised when Frank came roaring up in front of him — not two feet away.

Fists hammered at his chest and jaw; he weaved and dodged and ducked, came up — by pure chance — inside Frank's arms and drove the top of his head up under Frank's jaw. Teeth clashed together and blood oozed from

Frank's split lips. His eyes almost crossed with the pain, but he reached out blindly; his hands fastened on Wade's ears.

Yancey bawled in agonized pain and reached up to break the grip. Frank kneed him in the lower belly and he started to double up, the motion bringing more pain to his ears as Greer pulled and twisted relentlessly. His teeth were bared and his fingers couldn't break the terrible grip; it was as if Frank wanted to tear his ears completely off his skull.

Frank was trying his best to do exactly that!

The pain was driving him crazy; Wade jerked his head from side to side and tried to ignore the increased agony. He moved his body at the same time, pulling Greer after him — or forcing him to release his grip. No such luck! Frank hung on, his big blood-smeared teeth bared, eyes bulging in their sockets with the madness of imminent murder.

Swift as a striking snake, Yancey Wade's right hand drove up and out, fingers forked as they sought those mad eyes.

Too late, Frank realized he was in danger of being blinded and although he leapt back — releasing Wade's ears as he did so, the fingernails tore his eyelids and searing pain surged through the sockets.

Sobbing with the agony, Frank clawed at his own face. His vision was blurred, and he lurched to one side, partly crouched in an effort to escape. Legs shaking with exertion, Wade planted his boots as solidly as he could, then reached up almost in slow motion to twist his fingers in Frank's long, tangled, black hair. He wrenched as if he would scalp Greer, making him cry out in pain-driven fury.

Hardly knowing what he was doing, his hands and aching muscles seeming to move of their own volition, Wade lifted Greer off his feet and swung him in a short, violent arc, against the roughly stacked pile of planks.

The effort dropped Yancey to his knees and his head hung, sweat and blood dripping to the ground as Frank's body struck the piled timber hard enough to splinter one of the smaller planks and set the others rocking.

Then the whole pile collapsed and Greer's body disappeared into the spilling planks and frames, one leg poking up here, an arm there, the other at an odd angle.

Wade knelt there, staring through his own veil of agony and misted vision. He was just able to hear, through the roaring in his head, Walt bawling orders.

'For God's sake get Frank out. He'll be killed!'

As Wes and Tex Lyle rushed forward, Bugs Tyrell said grimly, 'I reckon that was the general idea.'

Mattie ran up and looked horrified: whether at Frank's predicament or Tyrell's words wasn't clear.

'Walt!' she cried. 'Can't you stop this? I — I've seen wild animals who wouldn't treat each other in such a manner.'

Wade didn't have any breath to spare

for an answer. Frank Greer was unconscious as the others threw the planks off his twisted body and dragged him into the open.

Walt Dedman looked from one bloody man to the other, then said curtly to Mattie, 'Could you tend to this pair of fools, Mattie?' He added quickly, 'If it's too much to ask, I'll send someone into town for the doctor. They could do with one, I think!'

'I once had to tend two men caught in a cattle stampede,' Mattie said, a mite breathlessly, her face pale. 'They didn't look much worse than this.' She straightened her shoulders, making no attempt to hide her disgust.

Wade could see her face only vaguely: one of his eyes was swollen almost shut. He would have liked to make some flippant remark but his cut and swollen tongue wouldn't pronounce the words. All he did was give a moaning, gargling sound before he passed out.

11

'Know When You're Beat!'

Walt Dedman watched Mattie poke the bloody rags and wads into the red coals glowing in the big kitchen's wood-fired range. Smoke swirled and the stench was strong before they finally burst into flames. Her hands were noticeably shaking.

'Sorry you had to get caught up in that, Mattie, my dear.'

She turned her head quickly. 'Walt, please don't call me 'my dear'! The way you say it — well, it makes you sound so — old. And it makes me feel that way, too.' She flushed as soon as she had spoken, then forced a smile, fitting the iron lid over the burning rags. 'I'm sorry. I didn't mean that, Walt. I — I think I'm a little more shaken than I realized. Both those men have such brutal injuries.' She looked pale, weary from her efforts.

He knew she had deftly turned the subject of his age away from her remark; he was aware that the difference in their ages — some twenty-six years — concerned the girl. Once again he silently cursed himself for having thoughtlessly taken for granted that she would accept his romantic approaches; after all, she was a lonely woman and had endured a hard life. Surely she should be glad of the attentions of such a man as himself? Not that there was any self-conceit involved in his thinking: only that he was on the verge of making a real success of his life at last, and could offer her security, an easier life, and plenty of love.

He had made the mistake of thinking she would snatch at the first decent offer so as to escape her drudgery. But he had underestimated her and her loyalty to her immature brother. She had been kind enough to allow him to make allusions to the possibility that they would eventually wed, hadn't actually discouraged him, while not — he realized now — encouraging his attentions. She was a kind person and — his heart fluttered as the thought came to him — perhaps she felt *sorry* for him. That shook him; it was the last thing he wanted. But he cleared his throat and said:

'I'm afraid we're dealing with very hard men here, Mattie.'

She nodded, washing her hands and forearms now over a tin bowl of disinfectant-clouded water. 'Yes, indeed. *Very* hard men, Walt. But I — I feel that Yancey Wade, even if he's involved with them, is not entirely . . . willingly so.'

Dedman frowned. 'Deep down, I believe I think so, too. But in the light of what Josh Cameron told us, well, we have to walk very carefully; they all had a hard war. And from what Cameron said peace hasn't been all that kind to any of them. Many such men have taken desperate measures merely to stay alive — risking their necks to do so.'

'That could be their own choice, of

course, but Walt, there isn't a lot we can do, is there? We don't know for sure that they're planning anything illegal, as Cameron implied.'

'No we don't, but going on what he *did* say, it's aroused my suspicions. I believe that's enough for us to tread warily. Especially where the Sundown Run is concerned.'

She dried her hands and picked up a small cotton bag that held more bandages, the stained cork of an iodine bottle showing above the edge. He smiled faintly, took her arm and walked to the door with her.

'I hope I'm wrong, 'specially about Yancey, but we have to be very wary, my . . . Mattie. Our whole future depends upon it. We need to be accepted as an important stageline stop-over. A robbery, even an attempted robbery, of the first stage through here would kill all that.'

'What will you do about the progress reports now that Cameron has refused to take them?'

Walt scowled. 'Petty behaviour! Never mind, with some luck the reports may even be there at Fiddler's Green head office before he gets back.'

Mattie frowned. 'What? How can . . . ?'

Walt smiled then. 'As far as I can make out, the Western Union linesmen reached a point about ten miles from here before the prairie fire wiped out their stock of poles and wire. They're able to stay in contact by hooking up to the wire already strung, as it's connected to the main grid. I know how to use a telegraph key, so I thought, if I ride out there I can wire the reports in. Then Cameron's pique won't delay things any more.'

Mattie brightened. 'That's a good idea, Walt. And Fiddler's Green will no doubt appreciate it.'

'The — er — patients will be all right? I mean, you can handle things until I get back? It's not really far.'

'Yes, I can manage. It may not be far, Walt, but you do have a mountain range to cross. It's very steep.' She paused and added, quietly, 'You could take Jason. He knows that range well, has searched for mavericks there. And the responsibility of guiding you will be good for him.'

Walt fought to keep his face normal, but inwardly he was far from ecstatic about a couple of days' ride with the surly Jason as companion. He cleared his throat.

'I'm not sure that it's necessary, Mattie, but, well, see what the boy says, eh?'

★ ★ ★

Wade came to in the cubicle that served as the way station's room for the head wrangler. At least it provided some privacy, but he thought you wouldn't want to swing a cat here by the tail — unless you didn't like cats and wanted to knock its brains out.

Wade's mouth tasted like a cesspool, or as he imagined a cesspool would taste: he had no personal experience.

159

He swallowed, grimacing as much from the effort it took as from the lousy taste. He moaned involuntarily, as he tried to hitch himself around to a more comfortable position. His muscles were not just aching-sore, but throbbing, pounding, with each beat of his heart. His body felt like it was tearing itself to pieces — and he was barely moving! Hell!

He stiffened when he felt a cool hand lightly touch his forehead; he snapped one eye open: only one, the right one, came open all the way. The left was a puffy mess of dried blood and bruised flesh. He was able to recognize Mattie Groom, although if it hadn't been for the sun coming through the sole dusty window and backlighting her hair, he might not have realized it was her.

Whatever he tried to say by way of greeting came out as an unintelligible grunt. She smiled as she bent over him, some of her hair falling forward and touching his face. He gave an involuntary start, turning his head away, startled.

'Easy, Yancey. I'm afraid you're just a

mess of bruises and grazes and swellings. But you'll live, though your nose will have a noticeable lean to port.'

He grunted and she gave him a sip of water. It felt marvellous and he cleared his throat a few times before speaking. 'How does Frank look?'

She smiled faintly. 'Terrible. Worse than you.'

'Good!'

'You fight hard, Yancey, very hard.'

'Only way when the other feller's snake-mean.'

She nodded thoughtfully. 'We — Walt and I — we thought you two were friends.'

He lifted his right hand, which was blotchy with dabs of iodine over split knuckles, and rocked it back and forth. 'Sometimes yes, sometimes no. We go back a long way. Fought in the same platoon during the war.'

'Yes, Frank mentioned that. He was at pains to tell us how you won a medal, which you seem to have rightly deserved.' He made a deprecating gesture as she added, 'Frank was trying very hard to convince Walt that he had done the right thing by giving you the head wrangler's job.' She frowned slightly, adding, 'As if it was very important to *him*, Frank, I mean, that you stayed on in that position.'

He made no audible reply, and she said, her gaze silently interrogating him: 'You've obviously had a falling-out: a serious one.'

'Happens.' He held her gaze with his one good eye and she suddenly nodded jerkily. 'When Frank doesn't get his own way he turns kinda mean.'

'I think he's demonstrated that clearly enough.'

'I guess I — kinda pushed things, too.'

'I know I'm prying. But it was a very brutal fight and you've both taken a full day to come round properly. You probably don't even remember me treating you yesterday. Do you?'

He shook his head: 'You mean I've lost a whole day?'

'More like a day and a half. We were very worried that both of you might have a touch of concussion.' She leaned forward and looked more closely at his damaged eye. 'But I think you're coming back to normal and Frank regained consciousness a little while ago. We do have a vested interest in you both, you know.'

He frowned and slowly nodded.

She waited, but if she expected more of an answer she was disappointed. 'Well, if I'm still prying, it's because we don't know a lot about any of you, and that ex-marshal, Cameron, gave Walt and me much food for thought, without being too specific. Walt has a big responsibility to the stageline, you know. His whole future is tied up with it, so he has to tread very carefully.'

Wade nodded. 'I'm mighty grateful to Walt. You, too. I'm not noted for biting the hand that feeds me, Mattie. But sometimes things don't always work out as you'd like.'

'You're saying . . . '

'Just what I said and no more,

Mattie.' His throat and battered lips hurt from the talking. 'Might be best if I move on.'

Her own frown deepened; she felt more *secure* with Wade here. 'I'm not sure that would be necessary.'

'Could be best, though. Be even better if the whole bunch of us moved on, I guess, but I don't have much say about that.'

The way that damaged, disconcerting eye roved over her face gave her the impression he was trying to tell her something here, without actually putting it into plain words. But she couldn't quite grasp what. At last she said: 'I'll . . . ' *not 'we', he noticed*, 'miss you, Yancey, if you go.'

'I'll be sorry to leave. Reckon I could get to like it here. Long time since I've met really decent folk like you and Walt.'

'Then stay! I . . . we . . . '

'Best if I go.' There was a stubborness in him now.

She hesitated, not wanting to push too hard, but then asked: 'Do you have some conflict of interests?'

'You could call it that.'

'Can't you just walk away? I've always had the strong impression that you're very much your own man.'

'Like to think so, but this time it's kind of complicated. It's out of my hands, really.'

'You're being forced into something you don't really want to do. That's it, isn't it? You're unable to get out of this — trouble, or deal, whatever it is, and — '

'Leave it there, Mattie!' There was a touch of desperation in her voice and while it pleased him, as well as surprised him, he merely added, 'Just . . . leave it.'

'Yancey, rewarding you is a really big and important thing in Walt's life. He's waited a very long time for the chance. Please don't spoil it for him — or yourself.'

'I know, and I'm grateful. But by going, *he*'ll know just how much I do appreciate what he's done.'

'Damn you and your riddles, Yancey

Wade!' Her gaze flicked over his battered face. 'I believe you're basically a good man. I don't pretend to understand what's going on, or perhaps I'm afraid to come to what seems like the inevitable conclusion.' She paused and took a deep breath. 'But I have the feeling you're putting yourself in a very dangerous position by doing this.'

'Most of my life I've been in danger of one kind or another.'

'But Frank Greer! He seems so — menacing.'

'He's very tough, very hard. Always has been. I think Frank and me are long overdue for a square-off — with guns.'

'Any time you say, Yancey, old pard.'

Mattie actually jumped as she gasped and spun quickly towards the narrow entrance door a couple of feet behind her. 'What're you doing out of bed?' she demanded.

Frank Greer stood there, or not exactly stood, for he leaned his shoulders against the doorframe, swaying a little. His cocked six-gun added to the menace he radiated.

His face was cut, distorted with swellings and bruises, his bandaged nose was set with plaster strips, another bandage was wrapped right round his head, covering one ear. Both eyes glittered dangerously from way back in bruised sockets.

'Glad to see you lookin' so poorly, Yance,' he said sourly. 'Not that I made a special visit to see you.' He turned to Mattie. 'Walt's back. Got the kid with him.'

Mattie smiled. 'That's good to hear.' She looked at him levelly. 'Do you need that gun?'

Frank flicked his eyes to Yancey, staring hard, then suddenly twirled the Colt around the trigger guard and let it drop back into his holster. 'Not right now. 'Less you got other ideas, Yance?'

Wade gestured with one hand, the fingers stiff and swollen. 'I know when I'm beat, Frank.'

'The hell you do! That's always been your trouble: you never knew when to give up.'

Wade glanced briefly at Mattie, then

167

back to Frank. 'This time I do.'

Frank smiled as he looked at the girl. 'You better.'

'Where'd Walt go, Mattie?' Wade asked, though still looking at Greer.

'He rode to the Western Union camp to wire through those reports that Cameron refused to take with him to Fiddler's Green.'

Wade nodded. 'Yeah. Cameron was sure miserable, actin' that way.'

'It certainly wasn't the kind of thing you'd expect from a United States marshal, retired or not.'

Her voice trailed off as she remembered how she had had to work to convince Dedman that taking Jason out to the Western Union camp would be good for the boy. Hard work!

Walt hadn't made it all that easy, either. He was preoccupied with getting his things together and hadn't seemed to be really listening to what she was saying:

'Oh, Walt, he's young and not very mature, but I know by the way he's acting that he's not happy having to live with those hardcases. I'm sure it would make him feel better, feel *wanted*, if he rode with you. You could say you needed him to show you the best way over the range: something *responsible*, that would boost his confidence, Walt?'

She had followed him around as he collected his papers and put them into his valise. Eventually she'd worn him down.

He was reluctant but at heart he was a compassionate man; he even admitted to himself that probably she was right: Jason did need something to restore his self-confidence.

So, with a sigh of resignation, Walt had smiled and said levelly, 'As you wish, Mattie. We'll probably just stay overnight.'

Her lips brushed his cheek. 'You're a kind man, Walt Dedman. Jason means a lot to me. He's my only kin and I dearly want to see him make a success of ranching. I'm sure his riding with you on what he knows to be important

169

business will do him good.'

Walt smiled. 'As you wish my de — er — Mattie. I'll see what I can do to put him at his ease.'

★ ★ ★

Now they were back and she couldn't wait to learn how the ride had gone . . .

12

Western Union

The first few miles had passed without either Walt or Jason saying much. They had to climb the steep mountain behind their ridge and it took quite an effort, zigzagging their mounts all over the rising slopes. At first Jason had merely ridden on ahead, leaving Walt to follow. Then he slowed and, almost side by side, they climbed, Jason silently making gestures as to the best way. Then his pinto almost tumbled down the steep grade, taking the boy with it, when, riding too close to the edge of the trail, the ground gave way.

Jason yelled, stood in the stirrups as he hauled rein on the frightened horse. Walt was slightly above, he hipped in the saddle and swiftly shook out a loop in his lariat. He flung it; Jason put up an arm and let the loop tighten under his crooked elbow, clinging firmly with his knees as he worked the reins with his right hand. It kept the pinto from falling, and its instinctive scrabbling, plus the riders' efforts eventually brought it back safely on to the trail.

After the frightened pinto had settled down, Jason stared at Walt. 'Never figured you'd know how to do that.'

'Oh, there's a lot you don't know about me, Jace,' Walt said, coiling his rope again and draping it over the saddle horn. 'I grew up in Wishbone, a cattle town on the trail to Abilene. Rode with several big herds, Charlie Goodnight's mainly, lived as a cowboy for years before I got into the stageline business.'

Interest showed in Jason's young, dust-smeared face. 'You worked at bein' a cowboy? For Charlie Goodnight?'

Walt smiled ruefully as he scratched at a couple of days' stubble on his jaw. 'Seems a long, long time ago now. I was intending to come down to the ranch and help out when time allowed me to leave the way station in your sister's charge. Sort of keep my hand in, you know. Maybe we'll still do that, once things're running smoothly.'

Jason was silent for the rest of the climb. At the top, while they rested the horses, he said, out of the blue, almost blurting the words: 'Walt, I din' think you were interested in me.'

Dedman smiled. 'Why wouldn't I be? I'm still hoping we'll be brothers-in-law.'

Jason sobered. 'Well, I dunno how Mattie feels . . . '

'No. I think I may've made a mistake in my excitement at being appointed way station manager-agent for Fiddler's Green. Tended to rush her off her feet and now she's having second thoughts.' He spoke soberly, then smiled. 'Well, there's a little while yet before it's settled, one way or another.'

They rode on, then hauled rein, and from the crest of the next and last rise they stared out at a vast black area smearing a series of small hills that trailed off into heat-hazed open country. Only a few stark trees remained upright, pointing at the sky like an old man's gnarled fingers.

'I guess that's what's left after the prairie fire,' opined Walt.

'It must've been a humdinger!'

'Aye.' Dedman shaded his eyes, though he still squinted. 'You can just make out the last pole they'd set, even glimpse the trailing wires with the sun shining on them.' He raised himself in the stirrups. 'Those look like tents, way off to the left there, beyond the burned area. That'd be the linesmen's camp, I guess. Closer than I figured.'

'How long will it take them to bring the line to the way station? Once they get replacement poles and wire, I mean?'

Walt shook his head. 'Hard to say. During the war they set all kinds of records, stringing wire on erected poles at the rate of about ten to twelve miles each day. Of course they had huge

174

teams of men working then, most supplied by the army. I don't know how many they have now. I seem to recall Cameron saying something about sixteen, but that's likely a bare minimum when you consider the work they have to do just to get one pole up: trim the pole, dig a hole, bolt insulators in position, string the wire and raise the lot.' He lifted his reins abruptly and touched his heels to the flanks of his mount. 'C'mon. Let's go see for ourselves.'

Jason spurred past him, yelling, 'Race you!'

Walt, caught napping, set his horse after Jason, saying aloud, 'Well, I'll be damned! The boy's human after all!'

★   ★   ★

The boss of the linesmen was a big, hard-bitten man with tufts of grey hair showing beneath his hat. His name was McNamara but everyone seemed to call him 'Poley'.

Jason, curious, asked one of the tough-looking linesmen, 'Why do they call him 'Poley'?'

The man looked at him, ran his tongue along the edge of his cigarette paper, rolled it deftly between thumb and fingers and stuck it between his lips. He fired up a match and lit it before answering.

'That's how he makes his livin'. Stickin' poles up all over the country and hangin' wire from 'em. He's the champeen poler in the whole of the Western Union outfit.'

'He looks mighty powerful.'

'Seen him lift a twelve-foot pole that'd pinned a man when a storm blew it down. Tossed it aside like a cigarette butt, then carried the hurt man half a mile to the camp. Never even raised a sweat.'

Jason took that with a grain of salt and turned his attention to Walt, who was now talking to Poley McNamara on the other side of the campfire.

'Yeah, Walt, you can send your

reports through to Fiddler's Green by our own hook-up.' Poley's voice was surprisingly light for such a tough-looking *hombre*. 'Have to ride a couple miles, though. Fire wiped out our two last poles here, so we had to send Banjo, our telegraphist, and a coupla men back to where the line was undamaged. They've got a bit of a camp there and Banjo's linked up with the wire carryin' the power. Lucky we salvaged a couple sulphuric acid battery jars for his key. But set you down and have some coffee and biscuits.' He scratched his head under his hat, only lifting it an inch or so, and ran his tongue over his lower lip. 'Best we can offer, but I tell you, I'd give a week's pay for a hunk of beefsteak.'

'Oh?' Walt asked, caught by surprise.

'Yeah, that damn fire wiped out our cows. They weren't quick enough to get away.' He swept one muscular arm around. 'There was a thick stand of timber right in the camp — in fact it's why we chose the spot in the first place.

There were some tall, straight pine trees we could've used for telegraph poles. Man, did they burn! Damn well exploded with all the resin an' sap in 'em. Poor damn cows never stood a chance; we had to bust our britches to save ourselves. Lost all our gear wagons; just had to watch 'em burn.'

'I can't do much about them, Poley, but I can get you some more cattle. Say, twenty, twenty-five. That do?'

'Man, you got a deal! Name your own price. Western Union don't stint on their workmen at times like this.'

Walt saw Jason on the other side of the campfire and lifted a hand. 'You hear, Jace?' When the boy nodded, he added, 'When we get back, pick a couple of men and drive the cows back here . . . ' He let the words trail off as he saw Jason's face hardening, realized he had been presumptious. 'Well, I guess that part's up to you. You're the rancher, but you'll need to round 'em up and so on. Shouldn't take you long, should it?'

'I'll see about it when we get back.' Jason spoke a bit curtly and McNamara arched his eyebrows as the boy turned and walked to where some of the other men had gathered.

'Mite touchy, ain't he?'

Walt smiled ruefully. 'Feeling his way, but he'll make good. When do you expect your replacement supplies to arrive?'

'Any time now.'

It was Walt's turn to arch his eyebrows. 'Quick work isn't it? I mean it's a long way back to Lacey and by the time they hire wagons and teams, then load up . . . ?'

Poley took a long, last drag on his cigarette, then ground the butt out under his boot. 'Comin' by rail.'

'Rail! What rail?' Walt blinked in his surprise.

Poley gestured to the low, blackened hills. 'The old Bonnet Creek railroad's just over them hills.'

'I've heard about it, but I understood it was abandoned years ago when the gold cut out at the Sunbonnet mine.'

McNamara grinned, revealing stained teeth with at least two missing. 'Western Union's a mighty powerful company, Walt. Some office-Jack up in head office remembered the railroad, figured it would be easier and faster to ship the replacement gear that way. It's within a half-mile of where the fire began and some of our good wire still stands. The train'll bring new wagons, with the poles and spools of wire already loaded on 'em. All we have to do is hitch the teams and drive 'em away. We still got plenty of hosses — they sure knew how to get away from the flames! So all we have to do is go meet the train and we're back in business.'

'Western Union got permission to reopen the line?'

'Yep — with a little help from Fiddler's Green. The railroad had gandy-dancers and teams of men workin' within a couple of days. We'll have your way station hooked up and operational within a week, maybe less, with a little luck.'

'We-ell. That mountain is much

steeper than it looks,' Walt said slowly, not wanting to dampen the man's enthusiasm too much.

Poley gave him a knowing smile. 'Never was WU's intention to string wire over the mountain, you know.'

Walt blinked. 'Then how can . . . ?'

'There's a cutting at the western end of the range.'

'Oh, yes, I know, but you can't get wagons through there; at some time an avalanche half-filled the cutting with boulders, they tell me.'

Poley squared his shoulders and managed to look quite proud. 'That's why we're blastin' 'em clear. Almost done, matter of fact.' At Walt's barely concealed scepticism, he added: 'We got the best dynamite men outside of the Union Pacific workin' for us. You see: we'll come a'thunderin' through with your poles and wire and we'll string 'em clear up into your parlour if you want. How's that sound?'

Walt smiled. 'Mighty good, Poley! Might-ee good!'

13

The Ranch

Jason Groom rode slowly into the ranchyard, frowned when he saw it was deserted.

All the horses were in the corrals, saddles on the rails. The timber for finishing the bunkhouse was still piled untidily in the yard. None of it had been used.

There was no sign of the men.

He dismounted slowly at the small corral, looped the reins around the middle rail and thumbed back his hat as he heard voices coming from inside the older section of the bunkhouse. He frowned. Then his lips tightened and he strode swiftly across, pushed the half-open door all the way back and stood there, glaring at the men sitting around the table, playing cards.

There was a half-empty, cut-glass decanter of whiskey in the middle of the table.

'What the hell's all this?' Jason snapped, annoyed that his voice rose a little too high-pitched,

The men glanced up: Bugs Tyrell, Tex Lyle, and even Wes Toohey. All had a slight glaze to their stares.

'Hey! Jace! Where you been?' said Bugs, but his eyes were suddenly hard.

'Never mind where I've been!' Jason made himself get mad now. He knew he had to show them who was boss, but inwardly he was afraid he wouldn't be able to carry it off.

But he tried. 'Why aren't you working? I can't see a damn thing that's been done since I've been away.'

Bugs leaned back in his chair, placing his hand of cards on the edge of the table. He ran his eyes over his companions and said, with a crooked smile: 'No peekin'!' Then he stood and faced Jason. 'You went off without tellin' us. We figured if you could take yourself a damn holiday, so could we.'

Jason flushed. 'It was no holiday! I had to ride out to the Western Union camp with Walt.' He stopped abruptly and realized it would be better if he didn't make too much of an explanation. 'And what's that decanter of whiskey doing here? You've damn well been inside my house!'

By then Bugs was leering around at the others. 'Hear that? Takin' a nice ride in the country, expectin' us to sweat and bust our backs out here!' Bugs shook his head and walked over to Jason. He raised one hand and waved a finger in the boy's taut face.

'That ain't how we're used to workin', Jace! An' we needed a drink. You weren't around to ask permission, so . . . Hell! Not like it's crystal! Only glass — '

Jason stepped back. 'Don't you talk back to me like that!'

'No? Well, tell you what. Me, I'm a man always figures actions are better'n words.'

Wes Toohey came swiftly to his feet. 'Cut it out, Bugs! He's the boss, dammit!'

'Yeah? Well I don't aim to be bossed around by no wet-nosed kid.' Bugs suddenly stepped forward, crowding Jason, who started to move back.

Then Bugs hit him just above the belt, a hard right driving into Jason's ribs on his left side. The younger man gasped, staggered and Bugs moved after him.

Wes Toohey started forward, but Tex Lyle stood up right in front of him, spread a hand against Wes's chest and shook his head. 'Leave it, Wes!'

Toohey stopped, frowning, watching as Bugs hit Jason again, in the lower ribs, pinning him against the wall. Jason was gasping, unsteady on his feet. His hat had fallen off; Tyrell reached out and grabbed a fistful of his red hair with his left hand, yanked the contorted face upwards.

'Trouble is, kid, you don't get it. *You* ain't the boss here. We run things to suit us, just killin' time till we're — '

'*Bugs*!' shouted Toohey. 'Shut up, you damn fool!'

Tyrell didn't like that, but he glared and said, 'All I was gonna say was till we're needed elsewhere. Anythin' wrong with that?'

Wes glared, shook his head. 'Guess not. But leave the kid alone. Walt or his sister must've told him to go to the Western Union camp. He wouldn't do it of his own accord.'

Bugs snorted, curled a lip and turned Jason's hair loose. The boy staggered, then fell to his knees. For a moment Wes and Tex thought Bugs was going to lift a knee into the boy's face, but the whole point of hitting him in the midriff was so no marks would show where they could be seen.

'Hey, kid! You with us? You get the picture now? You don't go nowhere without tellin' us first. That ain't too hard to remember, is it?'

Jason's mouth was distorted with pain and he shook his head slowly, embarrassed to admit even to himself that he was afraid of these men, simply wasn't capable of going up against them.

'Wh — what're you up to?' he managed to gasp, putting one hand out against the wall to steady himself.

Wes eased him into a chair. 'We're just here to help you out till Walt gets his way station up and runnin'. Ain't that right, boys?'

Tex looked to Tyrell for a lead and Bugs, eyes narrowed, nodded curtly.

'That's right, kid. But you gotta remember, we're men who've been ridin' the grubline for years, know about all there is to know of livin' from job to job. We ain't used to bein' bossed around by a spoiled kid like you.'

'I — I never bossed you — '

'Enough!' Bugs snapped. He reached for the whiskey decanter, taking a quick swig, spilling liquid over his stubbled chin and shirtfront. 'You just stick around and tell us before you decide to go off someplace an' you'll have no trouble. Savvy?' Jason nodded, surly, ashamed of his own cowardice. Bugs leered: 'We really like your company, kid. Ain't that right, fellers?'

'Don't overdo it!' growled Toohey.

Bugs started to lift the decanter towards his mouth again but Tex snatched it from him. 'Don't hog it all!'

As he took a long swig Bugs glared, then turned suddenly to Jason, making him jump. It pleased Tyrell to see the fear on the kid's face and he suddenly clapped him on the shoulder.

'I think you got our message, kid. Just you make sure you remember it. And remember your sister, too. Huh?'

Jason froze. 'Mattie? Wh — what's she got to do with this?'

'Nothin', kid, nothin',' Wes Toohey said before Tyrell could answer. He stared hard at Bugs. 'None of this is necessary. Would've been better if you'd never started it.'

'Yeah? You want me to start somethin' with you?'

Wes lifted one hand. 'Take it easy. Get that burr out from under your saddle. We've had a couple days easy-livin', ain't we? Not like we broke our backs while Jace was off with Walt.'

Even Tex Lyle nodded agreement. 'Think we should . . . kinda let it ride, Bugs. Frank'll be riled if we stir things up.' He nodded again at Jason. 'You know . . . ?'

Bugs did know, realizing he might've made Jason more suspicious of them than he'd been before. He suddenly grinned and started brushing down the boy's clothes.

'Hey, I guess I was soreheaded, kid. I been losin' at cards, and a few drinks sometimes get me riled. Listen, you take a drink?' He offered the now nearly empty decanter to Jason, who shook his head.

'It — it makes me sick if I drink on an empty stomach.'

Tex smothered a laugh but Wes nodded slowly, glaring at the now sneering Bugs, who shook his head sadly.

'Judas *priest*!'

'Why don't you go get washed up,

Jace?' Wes suggested quickly. 'Then we'll rustle up some grub for lunch.'

Jason ran a tongue around his dry lips, nodded, took his hat, which Tex held out to him, then turned and lurched away towards the door, one hand rubbing his sore midriff.

He stopped halfway and spoke over his shoulder. 'We've got to round up some cows later.'

'Yeah!' rasped Bugs. 'Much later! Go dunk your head, kid.'

Jason started to say something, then went out of the door, unsteady on his feet.

'That was a damn fool play, Bugs!' Wes said quietly.

'I was you, old man, I'd leave it right there.' Tyrell had switched the decanter to his left hand; his right hand was now resting on his gun butt.

Wes nodded slowly. 'Was . . . aimin' to do that.'

Bugs grinned evilly. 'Yeah. Always figured you was a man with good sense.'

190

Jason's mid-section was purple and blue with overlapping bruises and it hurt to breathe deeply. He swore — but at himself for not standing up to Bugs Tyrell.

He felt sick to his stomach; he'd never been aggressive and had had few fights during his schooldays. Big sister Mattie had somehow always been within reach to rescue him from bullies or other kids making fun of him because he was so much quieter than the average exuberant schoolboys. Although he was glad of her intervention, at the same time he resented it because it gave the others something else to tease him about.

'*Where's your big sister, Jay-son?*'

'*You won't be able to hide behind her skirts for ever, you big sissy!*'

'*Why don't you learn to fight. I'll give you a bloody nose an' see if you hit back — or just stand an' cry.*'

'*Yay! Cry-baby Jay!*'

He shuddered at the memories, and

he knew he *had* depended too much on Mattie, even in the years since he had left school: she was still very protective of him.

'Dammit! I — I'm gonna ask that feller Wade if he'll show me how to fight — or use a gun. He seems more approachable than any of the others. Except maybe Wes, but he's with Greer's men . . . '

He didn't even consider asking Walt, even though Dedman had shown a tougher side than Jason had imagined.

But — shaking as he had the thought — he wasn't going to let Bugs Tyrell or his pards humiliate him again.

And it still puzzled him why Bugs had told him to be sure to 'remember' Mattie.

It just didn't make sense.

14

The Telegraphist

When Walt Dedman came into the room being used by Wade, he found him soaking his swollen hands in a bowl of hot water. Wade glanced up and nodded.

'Come on in, Walt.' His words were slurred because of his swollen and cut mouth. 'Hear you've been out to Western Union's camp.'

'Yes. The gear that was lost in the fire will be replaced in a couple of days and we'll soon be operational.' He paused and nodded at Wade's hands. 'Look mighty sore.'

'Frank has a hard head. Should've known better and concentrated on his body more.'

Walt gave him a steady stare. 'It's over, I trust?'

'For now.' Wade's gaze back was just as steady.

'No. *It's over,* Yancey. I want no more fighting.'

Wade merely nodded, added a little more hot water from the big iron kettle on the floor.

'We've an important job to do and I want it to run smoothly. I hope you soaking your hands means no more than alleviating the pain?'

'Need 'em supple if I'm gonna work.'

Walt still looked very sober. 'Work's fine. As long as you're aiming to hold tools and not a gun.'

'Tools are what I had in mind, Walt. But it's nice to know my hands'll work smoothly if I do need to hold a gun. Only if Frank's goin' for his, of course.'

Dedman heaved a sigh. 'All right. I know you two are still enemies, but I warn you: any differences you still have with Frank Greer, settle them in your own time, and not on my way station.'

'OK by me. Might be as well to let Frank know, too.'

Walt nodded curtly. 'Can you ride?'

'I've been stiffer and achin' more after bustin' a slew of broncs. Yeah, I can ride. Mebbe better after I take it easy for another day, but I can do it whenever you want. You got something in mind?'

Walt told him about the Western Union camp needing beef. 'It can be supplied quite easily from Mattie's ranch, and give Jason his first real income. But he's not experienced in round-up, nor in many ranch duties, for the matter of that, and — well, I don't really care for the men we've left with him.' He paused, looking expectant, but Wade kept his battered face blank. 'Could you ride on over and kind of supervise? See that . . . well, things go smoothly?'

Yancey nodded. 'I can do that. They might be hard-cases, Bugs and Tex, but they know ranch work, and Wes is a top hand. But, yeah, I'll go. When did you have in mind?'

'Will tomorrow be too soon for you?'

195

'A week would be too soon, mebbe. But best if I get moving quick as I can. No sense in sittin' around, growing stiffer.'

'Then it's settled?'

Wade nodded. 'I'll watch out for him, Walt.'

'I'm much obliged, Yancey. Mattie will be pleased, too.'

★ ★ ★

'Hey, Walt!'

Dedman was checking the windows in the passenger overnight section and turned sharply at the harsh voice.

Frank Greer came limping up, his battered face set in angry lines. 'What's this I hear about Yancey goin' to help round up some cows? Hell, I got three good men over there've been livin' and sleepin' with cows for years.'

'I want Yancey to teach Jason.'

'Christ, Bugs or Tex can do that; even Old Wes is no slouch. I just don't see the need for Yancey to . . .'

He limped up to within a few feet of Walt and stopped when he saw Dedman's face set in hard lines.

'You don't have to see it, Frank. You work for me and it's my decision. Anyway, you look as if you could do with another day or so resting up.'

Frank flushed, making his face appear blotchy. 'The hell I do! If Wade can set a saddle, so can I.'

'I want you to get some putty and a sheet of spare glass. There's a cracked windowpane that needs replacing.'

'Hell, Jason can do that. I want to — '

'You want to keep working here, Frank,' Walt cut in, 'you'll do what I tell you.'

Frank started to protest but bit off the hot retort, heaving a steadying breath, then grabbing quickly at his lower left ribs, which were sore from Yancey's fists. He nodded curtly. 'Yeah, OK, OK. Just seemed like sendin' Yancey . . . ' He broke off when he saw Dedman's face clouding and turned away. 'I'll go get the goddamn putty.'

Walt was turning out to be tougher than expected!

Mattie stepped out of a side door, a bucket of vegetable peelings in her hand, and watched Frank limp towards the toolshed.

'There's something strange about Frank and his men, Walt. Something that makes me uneasy.'

Dedman nodded, lighting a cheroot. 'Yes. I've had that feeling ever since I hired them — in my exuberation.'

'You're the one can hire or fire,' she pointed out.

'Yes. But I think I'd prefer to have these men where I can see them than . . . otherwise.'

Mattie glanced at him quickly. 'You think they're up to something?'

He smiled crookedly. 'That's my exact thoughts, Mattie. *Up to something.* I'm just not sure what.'

'Do you think Yancey is involved?'

Walt frowned. 'I don't know. I hope not.'

'So do I,' she murmured. She moved round him and carted the bucket towards her garden. Walt's frown deepened.

★   ★   ★

They rounded up twenty-five cows, not just the twenty ordered: Wade said there seemed little point in breaking up such a small herd for the sake of five extra beasts. Bugs and Tex watched but didn't offer to help. Wes Toohey cut out several small groups, then waved off Jason's thanks.

A day and a half later they were driving the herd towards the mountain range, just the two of them now, riding around constantly at first, until the well-fed cattle settled down and ambled along, so that the two men could afford to take it easier.

'Figured out how much you're gonna charge?' Wade asked Jason, riding up alongside the pinto.

'I'm not sure. How high d'you think I can push him?'

Wade put his mount closer to the boy's. 'You don't look at it that way. He might agree to pay twenty-five, thirty dollars a head because his men have been without beef for so long. But it'll be just a one-off. When he wants more beef, he'll think twice about what he paid you, and drop his offer way down — or go somewhere else. Might even feel he had been taken advantage of, the first time. Not a good thing to have folks sayin' about you.'

Jason frowned. 'I just thought — well, you know: kinda strike while the iron's hot — sort of.'

Wade looked at the boy's sweat-beaded face steadily. 'It's a whole lot easier to do the right thing; by that I mean, play fair. You'll find it comes out 'fair' all round in the long run and your reputation'll spread. A *good* rep.'

'Yeah, OK! I can see that. Guess I've got heaps to learn about runnin' a spread.'

'Knowin' that it is a good start.' Wade stood in the stirrups suddenly, squinting through the haze of dust raised by the small herd. 'What the hell?' He pointed and Jason shaded his eyes. 'Damn! Those can't be wagons.'

Jason nodded. 'I reckon so. But what're they doin' way down that end of the range? There's a kinda trail over the top, it zigzags and it's risky, but all the wagons use it 'cause it's the only one. Sure no trail that far along.'

'How about the cutting?'

Jason looked at him sharply. 'It's in that direction; can't see it for the mountain. But it's no place for wagons. They couldn't get past all the boulders blocking the pass.'

'Walt said Western Union were blasting 'em.'

'Yeah! That's what McNamara told him, but I don't know if they would've done it yet!'

'Unless those three wagons can sprout wings, I reckon it's the only explanation, kid.' Wade lifted the reins. 'C'mon. The herd'll shamble along quietly long enough for us to ride out and see what we have waiting for us.'

They spurred away from the easy-going cattle and rode fast towards the distant dust cloud raised by what Wade decided just had to be heavily-loaded wagons.

He was right. There were three of them, two flatbeds stacked with tele-graph poles ready for erection, and one covered wagon which likely hauled the camping-out gear and tools, and the heavy spools of wire.

There were two outriders. They lifted hands in greeting as Wade and Jason came in, hauling rein. Jason recognized the man he had asked about Poley McNamara's nickname and set his pinto alongside the other's dun.

'Didn't 'spect to see you again so soon.'

The man nodded, thumbed back his hat from his sweating forehead. 'Them powder-monkeys know their job. Only took seven charges and they cleared the main boulders blockin' the pass. Made a track wide enough for wagons.' He nodded towards the lumbering herd.

'And you fellers can save yourselves a climb by pushin' them cows through from this side. You'll have plenty of help once the boys back in camp hear them critters bawlin'.'

Jason continued to talk to the man, but Wade was riding from wagon to wagon, looking at the loads. He noticed one man on a covered wagon seat, squeezed between the driver and a second man, watching him closely.

He didn't know him but he seemed different from other Western Union men. His clothes were more like town-bought than the rough, patched outfits worn by the telegraph gang. The man lifted a tentative, gloved hand and Wade put his mount in close. He still didn't recognize him but it was obvious he wanted to speak with Yancey. 'Your name Wade by any chance?'

'I'm Yancey Wade. There something I can do for you? Or are you just admiring my warpaint?' He indicated the blotches made by the bruises, cuts and swabs of iodine, but he half-smiled when he said it.

The driver slowed the wagon as the man clambered over the third man on the seat and dropped to the ground. He was as tall as Yancey, but older and thinner. He had a long upper lip and his Irish face broke into a grin as the wagon rolled on by. He thrust up his right hand to Wade.

'Kinda suits you. 'Scuse the glove. Have to protect my hands. I'm Eric Case, one of Western Union's senior telegraph operators. On my way to the new way station.'

Yancey shook hands. 'No one expecting you this soon.'

'Guess not. But the line boss figured if I ride in with the workteam, I can set up all the internal paraphernalia, top up the battery jars and so on, have everything ready to hook up once they string the wire, which won't take long now they've made a trail through that cutting.'

'Well, I know Walt Dedman'll be happy to see you, Eric. He's a bit of a worrier, but I think he actually enjoys it, up to a point.'

'Know a few like that.' Eric Case glanced round at the first of the flat wagons. There were three horses tethered to the tailboard and he started towards them. 'I'll get myself mounted and ride with you a'ways.'

When he had chosen a mount, a big-chested roan, Wade signed for him to accompany him back to his drag position with the small herd. Brief, shouted introductions were made between Jason and Case and then Yancey and Case set their mounts behind the herd, keeping out of the dust as well as they could: Case used a bandanna to cover his mouth.

There was general talk for a spell, then most remarks were concentrated on the way station and its importance in the opening of the new stage trail.

'Fiddlers Green gonna use it for regular runs with their gold?' Yancey asked casually. It earned him a quick, penetrating look from the telegraphist.

'I dunno about their plans. My guess

is that if they have as much trouble as they did with the current run Fiddlers'll think twice about it. They're a powerful company, you know; they can dictate their own terms.'

Wade frowned. 'I thought the idea of opening this new run was to make it easier to get the gold to where it's s'posed to go? To the railroad at Lacey, wasn't it?'

'That was the idea. Aw, I guess they'll sort it out. Was Cameron who mostly caused all the fuss and delay.'

'He's s'posed to be their security man, he says.'

Case nodded. 'Not happy though. You know he resents being dumped by the marshals? No worthwhile backpay.'

'Yeah, he did a fair bit of bitchin' about it. Because of some old gunshot wound, wasn't it?'

'Bullet lodged close to his heart. Guess the Feds didn't want to risk him dying while he was still serving. They just had their annual appropriation for the marshals cut by Congress and the

206

insurance clause in Cameron's contract would cost 'em thousands if ever there was a claim.' Quickly he added ruefully, 'But I never told you that.' He winked. 'Being a top-grade telegraphist I see all that kinda stuff passing through. S'posed to keep it to myself.'

'Well, Cameron's a fool if he takes it out on Fiddlers Green. They must pay well, rich company like that.'

'Not as much as you might think, but they're pretty decent, bend the rules in deserving cases. No, Cameron has a mad-on at the whole damn world these days. But he's still got some integrity. As his last job — which no one knew it was — he set up the stage for carryin' the gold: designed a special bracket to hold a strongbox *inside* the rear seat. With strengthened springs to take the extra weight, it even makes the stage ride better. Did most himself, even made some parts of it, and oversaw the fitting. Passengers'll be sittin' on top of it and never know there's a fortune rubbing their backsides. I hear Fiddlers paid him a bonus of some kind, then he just up and quit.'

Wade's eyebrows shot up. 'Quit?'

Eric Case nodded. 'Yeah, said all the strain of getting things set up had taken its toll. He was feeling poorly, and he sure looked kinda pinched and pale, kept rubbing his chest. Anyway, like I say, he took his bonus and lit out. Just picked up his money and rode off without saying 'so long' to anybody.'

'Yeah, well he was always as rough as a cob, Josh Cameron. What made him such a good marshal before he caught that bullet, I guess.'

Case frowned slightly. 'You ever know him in — er — in an *official* capacity?'

Wade held his gaze. 'I ran into him a few times,' he said evasively, and Case nodded slowly.

'Well, he ain't toting no badge now. Should feel sorry for him, I guess. Kinda big let-down for him.'

'Sorry for Cameron?' Wade shook his head. 'Not me.'

Case studied his dusty face a spell

and nodded curtly. 'Well, anyone trying to steal the gold from that stage'll have to damn near take the whole thing apart to get at the strongbox, they say. He really earned that bonus.'

'Know when the stage's due through here?' Yancey asked as casually as he could.

Case didn't seem to notice any slight tension in his query. 'Well, I know they're stringing that wire night and day to make up for time lost in the prairie fire. Using carbide lights at night. Soon as it's hooked up, I give the word to Fiddlers and then it's up to them when they schedule the run.' He lowered his voice. 'I hear, on the quiet, it's waitin' already at Eton's Creek. Guarded like the President, too, but ready to go as soon as they get the word.'

Wade nodded. 'Guess the fire destroying all those poles and such set their schedules back because we weren't ready at this end. *Hey*!' Wade suddenly spurred after three breakaway steers, leaving Case blinking. Wade used his rope and his horse and a few choice words to get the steers back into the herd, then rode back to Case.

'You worked in Eton's Creek a while back, didn't you?' the telegraphist asked. 'Remember seein' you.'

Yancey snapped his head up at the question; he *had* been in Eton's Creek, planning a bank hold-up with Frank, but it never came off. 'I've passed through, coupla times,' he told Case warily.

'Thought I recognized you. Was me sent you that wire.' At Yancey's puzzled look, he added, 'I mean, I had the *job* of sending it.' When Yancey still didn't seem to understand, he said impatiently: 'About the boy in the sanatorium in Arizona. Damn! I hate sending such messages. Can't help but feel for the people they're goin' to. Felt damn sorry for you, too, if it means anything.'

By now, Yancey's stomach was knotted like a greenhorn's lariat. 'Why would you feel sorry for me?' he rasped. 'I never got any wire.'

The surprise on Case's face was

genuine, Yancey could see that. 'You didn't? Your friend Greer picked it up. Oh, Christ! Me and my big mouth. Then you don't know?'

'Know what?' Wade asked, barely audibly.

'About the boy. He died.'

15

Up For Grabs

'You'll have to get one of these other rannies to help you with the cattle. Something important's come up and I have to get back to the way station.'

Jason stared, his mouth partly open, at Wade's quick, harsh words. It was obvious the man was irritated. He started to speak as Wade lifted his reins and began to turn his mount.

'Hey, wait! Judas, Yancey, what the hell's happened?'

Jason sounded panicky as he jammed home his spurs, putting his pinto across the path of Yancey's black. There was a lot of whinnying and man-cussing, hauling of reins and, at last, a settling of the snorting, rolling-eyed mounts.

'Get outta the way, Jace!' Yancey snapped, fighting his still-prancing

212

mount. 'No time to explain. See Case! He'll get someone to help you.'

He spurred round the puzzled boy's mount and galloped back towards the distant way station.

★   ★   ★

There wasn't anybody in the yard of the way station, Yancey could see that as he galloped in. There were some men in the distance, clearing weeds from the edges of the new path they were grading from the stagecoach arrivals point, so the passengers had easy access to the stopover rooms.

He looked around quickly as the black skidded to a halt, blowing hard. Wade left the saddle fast, but overestimated his fitness and stumbled, falling to hands and knees. He got up, dusting off his clothes, as he saw Walt now, standing in the doorway of the reception area.

Dedman looked pale and tense. 'You all right, Yancey?'

'Yeah. How about you?'

213

Wade continued to move forward, then spun to his right as Frank Greer's voice said,

'Everyone's fine, Yance. An' they'll stay that way, long as they do what they're told. And that includes you.'

Wade's grip on his gun butt eased as Frank came round the corner holding Mattie tightly by her left arm, his Colt pressing into her side. 'Here's Mattie to say How-do!'

'Come on, Frank. No need for this.'

Frank laughed. 'The hell there ain't! I was watchin' through Walt's field glasses, curious to see how good the kid was at pushin' cows. Seen them wagons, and you havin' a lo-ong talk with some feller Bugs recognized as the telegraph operator from Lacey.' His smile and bantering tone disappeared. 'What'd he tell you that spooked you?'

Yancey had barely glanced at the pale, half-struggling girl, but spared her a brief look now; then he set his hard stare on Frank.

'You son of a bitch! Why the hell

didn't you give me that wire when you picked up the mail in Eton's Creek?'

Frank shrugged. 'Was goin' to, but when I seen what was in it, well, I figured it'd only upset you, mebbe take your mind off the bank business.'

Mattie stopped struggling and looked quickly from Frank Greer to Yancey. He was tensed like a coiled spring and she hoped his bleak, malevolent gaze was meant solely for Greer.

'And when we had to abandon the job? Why didn't you tell me then, about Terry dying?'

Frank shrugged. 'Figured it wouldn't do any good, only get you all riled up. Nothin' you could do, anyway.'

'But you used him as a threat to make me join you to rob the stage here! There never was a man just waitin' to kill Terry on your word, was there? You goddamn lyin' snake!'

Frank shrugged. 'We-ell, spur of the moment thing.'

Yancey was silent, still looking murderous. 'Let her go, Frank. Step

215

away and we'll finish this.'

Greer laughed. He shook the girl violently, making her hair fly around her face. 'Not right now. I still need you.' Frank shook Mattie briefly. 'See?'

Wade forced himself to calm down; his rage would make him vulnerable, the surging of his anger would drive him recklessly, maybe too recklessly. It could get Mattie killed. Walt, too. Bugs was standing beside Dedman now, holding a shotgun. Yancey knew Tex Lyle and Wes would be around somewhere: Frank would have them all ready.

'Forget the stage, Frank. Eric Case, the operator Bugs recognized, told me Cameron's last job was to make that coach like a bank vault on wheels. You'll never get the gold.'

'Cameron's *last* chore?'

Wade nodded. 'He took a bonus and quit, but not before making that gold nigh impossible to steal.'

'I like that word, 'nigh'.'

Wade shook his head slowly. 'Take you a week to even get the strongbox

out of the stage, let alone prise it open.'
Briefly, he told them what Eric Case
had said about Cameron making his
swan song one that would be remembered for years to come: the most secure
stagecoach ever to cross the prairie.

Frank was silent when he finished,
his face set hard. Then he tightened his
grip on Mattie's arm, bringing a small
cry of pain from her as she struggled.

'Shut up!' Frank snapped, shaking the
girl now. She subsided, the glisten of
tears on her high cheek bones making
Wade's trigger finger itch. 'When's the
stage due?'

'No one knows for sure.'

Frank swivelled his gaze to Walt, who
said, 'I can't tell you! We've had no
contact with Fiddlers Green, you know
that. The wires have to be strung first.'

'OK. Yance, when'll that wire get here?'

'Couple of days, I guess. You going to
keep us all prisoners that long?'

'Why the hell not? We've got the
place under control. Plenty of grub,
ammo. We can wait.'

He sounded confident and Wade knew Frank could do it, too.

'No guarantee when the stage'll come, Frank.'

'But it *will* come. We'll wait it out.'

'And find out you can't get at the gold without taking the stage apart, because of how Cameron rigged it.'

Frank's eyes seemed to blaze briefly in the deep, bruised sockets. 'There ain't a stagecoach made can stay in one piece after a couple sticks of dynamite. Nor any strongbox. An explosion won't hurt gold. No! Save your breath, Yancey! Nothin's changed. Just a mite delayed.' Frank's gun jerked suddenly. 'Now shuck your gunbelt. Or Missy here is gonna be short one of her toes.'

Wade, shoulders set rigidly, unbuckled his gun belt, let it fall at his feet, then moved away from it.

'Wes, go pick it up,' Frank ordered. Toohey stepped round Walt and Bugs, glancing briefly at Yancey, his face unreadable, as he collected the gunbelt and walked back to where Walt stood under Bugs's Colt.

'Where we gonna put 'em, Frank?' Tex Lyle asked, appearing in the kitchen doorway, munching a cold corn dodger.

'Root cellar.'

'Gonna be cramped. Lotsa cans and jars still in packin'-cases down there.'

'Hell, Tex, I don't care if they gotta stand on each other's shoulders. Just get 'em locked in!' Frank suddenly smiled and pushed Mattie roughly so that she sprawled in the yard. He made no move to stop Yancey helping the girl to her feet. 'Don't worry, Yance, you an' me'll settle up.'

'How about right now?'

Frank laughed, shaking his head slowly. 'You always was an eager beaver, Yance! No, *amigo*. I'll call the tune. Fact, I'm already callin' it. That tell you anythin'?'

*   *   *

It was cold and dank in the root cellar, and dark as the inside of a sealed coffin.

Only Mattie and Yancey were put down below. Frank wanted Walt with him for when the stage came. Yancey and Mattie huddled on one side of the racks of shelves that contained jars and cans and packages, as well as some fresh vegetables from Mattie's gardens. Conchita, the Mexican cook had been kept in the kitchen where the terrified woman was ordered to prepare a big meal for Frank and his men.

Wes Toohey brought the prisoners food: cold, but still appetizing left-overs from one of Conchita's meals served earlier in the day. Bugs stood with a shotgun at the top of the short set of steps leading up to the kitchen itself, warning Wes not to stand in the line of fire.

'Jus' serve 'em that slop and get on up here.' Bugs's words were slurred and Yancey knew he had been at Walt's supply of whiskey. 'Frank wants to give us orders for tomorrow.'

'*If* the stage comes,' said Wade.

Wes set down his load of food. He

could just make out Yancey's shape. 'Could it be that soon, Yance?'

'Mebbe. They're way behind schedule, so they just might push things.'

Wes whistled softly. 'Frank'll be happy.'

'Wes, is there a way out of here?'

'Hurry it up, Wes! You're like an old woman!' Bugs sounded angry and Toohey yelled,

'On my way, Bugs.' He added quietly to Yancey: 'Only way out is up them stairs, Yance. Enjoy your grub.'

He hurried back up and the blackness seemed blacker than ever as the trapdoor closed behind him.

'Might as well eat,' Yancey said, resignation sounding plain in his words as he groped for the tray.

The food was appetizing, though cold, some of it at least a day old. But they knew they needed sustenance, if not right now, certainly for what might lie ahead . . .

'Who was Terry, Yancey?' Mattie asked quietly, adding quickly: 'I know it's not really any of my business.'

Yancey's voice was tight as he spoke. He cleared his throat quickly. 'He was my sister Marian's kid.' He paused and Mattie groped in the dark for his hand. She squeezed it.

'If it's too painful . . . '

'It is painful, but won't hurt for you to know Marian's husband, Lew, was a gambler, ran out when she got pregnant. We had a small ranch left us by our father, but I had to take up trail-herdin' to keep it goin'. Came back one night from a really long drive and found Marian havin' the baby on the kitchen floor. It was birthin' hard and I guess I panicked. Took off for town to get the doctor.'

He paused and Mattie thought he wasn't going to continue, but he did so, very quietly. 'Like I said, it had been a long, hard trail drive and I'd celebrated the end of it with the boys. Took a wrong turning in the dark.'

Another pause. 'When I got back with the doc, the kid was — sort of born, but the birth cord had caught round his neck, restricted the blood supply and damaged his brain.'

'Oh! How awful!' Mattie gasped feelingly.

'He lived, but he was handicapped. Marian took care of him till he grew some but he could only speak slowly, and slurred, wasn't able to walk properly, needed help feedin', getting dressed, and would for the rest of his life. I could see it was gettin' her down.'

He paused and took a deep breath. 'He was a great kid and we struggled for a few years but it was really beyond us.'

'You stayed to help?'

'Yeah. If I hadn't took that wrong trail . . . '

Mattie's hand tightened on his arm. 'Oh, Yancey! You can't blame yourself for what happened.'

'I can, and do. But forget that part. In the end I knew we needed help. I heard about this professor in Montville, Arizona: he was developing a programme to help kids like Terry. Somethin' to do

223

with special exercises and food and herbal medicines. I was a bit sceptical but for Marian's sake I got in touch with him and he agreed to take Terry.'

'And did his treatment help?'

'There was some improvement but he'd warned we could never expect a full cure. Marian — well, she took to a kind of wild living, some sort of compensation for all the years of worry and struggle with Terry, I guess. Anyway, she couldn't face up to what might lie ahead, and she ran off with some drummer. That left me, all the kin Terry had. The professor needed a lot of money to keep going.'

There was a drawn-out silence again. 'I ran into Frank. Knew him from the army. He was ridin' the owlhoot with a small bunch and I decided to join him. Figured I could get the money for Terry quickly that way. It was a bit risky, but I had to have it. Well, I guess something must've gone wrong with the treatment. The professor had always warned it could be chancy.

'He sent a telegraph to me, care of General Delivery, Eton's Creek. Frank collected it with some other mail, it seems, and didn't tell me something had gone wrong, and Terry had died.'

'It must've been shattering for you!'

Wade didn't answer right away. 'Yeah. We were planning on sticking up the Eton's Creek bank at that time. Frank figured the news would hit me hard and maybe I wouldn't concentrate on the job.' There was a brief silence. 'Anyway we never robbed the bank — turned out to be too risky, and Frank decided I didn't need to know about Terry at all.'

He felt her hand on his arm again, aware of her closeness, her warmth, down one side of his body in the darkness. She jumped as he said abruptly, coldly, 'But I *do* know now. And I aim to kill Frank Greer.'

Mattie's hand clamped tightly on his arm as she drew down a deep, sharp breath at the bleakness of his words.

★ ★ ★

225

Frank Greer was concerned about Yancey, too. He knew what Wade was capable of when he applied his mind to it, so he ordered that the prisoners were to go hungry, to miss at least two meals, the trapdoor was to remain closed.

There was bright light showing through cracks where it didn't fit tightly and Yancey reckoned it was early afternoon on the second day. He hammered and banged on the door several times before Tex Lyle's voice drifted down.

'Get right away from the steps, Yancey! Right goddam away! Bugs is here beside me an' he's got the shotgun. We see you anywhere near the steps when I open up, even your shadow, and Bugs'll cut loose! Savvy?'

Wade knew what destruction a shotgun blast could cause in such a confined space. He shouted up that he would stand well back from the steps.

'Well, you do it, Yancey. We always got along tolerably well, you and me, but this is the big deal. No time for sentiment. You know I'll blast you if I have to.'

'I hear you, Bugs. We're right at the back, as far from the steps as we can get.'

'Stay there!'

Then the trapdoor lifted. Tex heaved it all the way open, then let the flap crash down. Dust and grit blew downwards in a choking cloud, causing Wade and the girl to cough briefly.

'Puttin' your grub on the third step.'

'Is Walt all right?' called Mattie quickly.

'Sure, sure,' Tex answered, letting the door drop back into place.

Mattie held Wade's arm as he started carefully to climb the steps. 'He didn't sound convincing!'

'Meant for you to think that, keep you worried.' He patted her hand. 'Walt'll be all right, Mattie. They need him for when the stage does arrive. Make things look normal.'

He didn't think she was convinced. She only picked at the food Conchita had prepared, and remained very quiet.

The day dragged without any further contact from Frank's outlaws — or anyone else for that matter.

Mattie was restless, vague in her replies to Wade's remarks, and he knew she was worried about Dedman. The roustabouts had probably been given a couple of dollars and told they could ride into town and paint it as red as the money would allow.

They were both dozing a little — Wade figured it to be around mid-afternoon — when suddenly the trap slammed back with a crash and they heard an excited woman's voice speaking in rapid Spanish, as if the words were being fired from a Gatling gun.

'Conchita!' Mattie breathed, looking up at the oblong of sky. The fat Mexican woman's shape appeared in the sunlight and then became a dark silhouette as she descended the steps, still speaking rapidly and loudly, throwing one arm about wildly.

'Stay back from them steps!' yelled Tex Lyle, appearing behind and above the cook. 'She needs some more flour or herbs or some damn thing. Now you hurry up and get it, señora. *Comprende? Mucho rapido!*'

The woman glanced up at Tex, giving him a mouthful of almost incomprehensible Spanish as she started to check the jars and cases. Apparently ignoring Wade and Mattie, she was unscrewing lids, taking out the ingredients she wanted, muttering all the time. She moved around the shelves towards where the hostages crouched.

'Hey, come back here, you fat bitch!' Tex bawled. 'You stay away from them.'

Conchita shook a fist and ignored the order, stepping into the shadowed part of the cellar. Then, with a scream she hit a stack of jars and carefully balanced wooden cases of bottles: sauces, flavourings, infusions of culinary herbs, and they tumbled down in all directions. She covered her face with her hands as she sprawled and rolled across the floor. Mattie and Wade dodged the tumbling, shattering cases and helped the Mexican cook halfway to her feet, dragging her back away from further danger.

'Goddamnit! You get back here where I can see you,' yelled Tex Lyle, starting down the steps.

Above, out of sight to those in the cellar, Bugs Tyrell called, 'What in hell's all that racket, Tex? Judas, man! You all right, *señora*?'

'*Sí! Sí!*' Conchita confirmed, close to Wade's ear as he helped her regain her balance. She reached down — to adjust one of her sandals that had twisted part-way off, Yancey thought — but suddenly she was pushing a six-gun into his hands. 'Here, *señor*. This much better than *frijoles*, eh?'

'Get down, Mattie!' Wade hissed as he took the gun. 'Stay here with Conchita.'

He dived suddenly to the side and Tex, halfway down the steps was startled: he swung his shotgun and fired. The shot shattered more bottles and splintered cases. Wade rose to his knees and triggered as Tex lunged back up the steps. The man swung the smoking shotgun down into the cellar as he reached for the trapdoor with his other hand.

He made a perfect silhouette against the afternoon sky. Yancey shot him twice. The outlaw staggered, trying to keep his balance. But he tumbled down the steps, the shotgun falling from his hands. Wade spun and spread his arms as he leapt and brought down both women. But the shotgun didn't discharge and Wade was thrusting upright and lunging for the weapon before they had recovered.

Another shotgun blasted above; the charge sent broken glass and pinewood splinters thrumming across the cellar.

Yancey twisted, got the Greener in the right grip and lay at an angle across the steps as he fired. At that moment, Bugs Tyrell chose to look down into the cellar to see what damage his own blast had accomplished.

Grimacing, ears ringing with the contained gunfire, Yancey leapt up, grabbed Bugs's gory figure and hurled him over the side of the steps into a patch of darkness.

'Come on!' he called in a raspy voice, reaching down for the near-hysterical

231

Conchita. He hauled her bulk up with a grinding effort. 'Watch the blood!' he snapped, and rolled her aside, then he lifted the much lighter Mattie bodily and set her on the ground.

There was chaos in the station yard.

The stagecoach must have been entering the yard when the gunfire in the cellar alerted the driver that something was wrong. He was Mitch Danner, and he was standing in his seat, swaying precariously, bent out to one side with the thick bunch of reins half-wrapped around his waist for leverage to saw at the slobbering mouths of the team. He hauled the coach away from the way station buildings and almost made it.

But Frank Greer appeared in the reception doorway, a rifle to his shoulder, and with his usual callousness, shot the two lead horses through their heads.

The crash was shattering as the heavy coach body rode up and into the struggling mass of the team's survivors. Someone was yelling — more than one man — and flailing arms appeared briefly at the windows as the coach crashed onto its side, spun and skidded. Frantically thrashing hoofs splintered the woodwork as the vehicle slid wildly and thudded into one end of the building, jarring the framework apart.

Yancey had snatched Bugs's six-gun from the dead man's holster and now began shooting fast. But even as tangled bodies tumbled out of the coach, dazed, and some injured, Frank reached behind him and dragged out a bloody-faced Walt Dedman, pulling the man quickly in front of him. He pressed the muzzle of his rifle up under Walt's ear, and grinned tightly at Wade.

'Best drop it, Yance!'

Breathing hard, Wade glanced at the bodies scattered across the yard, some moving painfully, a couple staggering upright, one or two lying there groaning.

'*Now!*' Frank gritted.

Wade let the smoking six-gun fall and lifted his hands out from his sides, swaying on his feet. The men who had been flung from the stage were helping each other up, and it registered with Yancey that there were no women passengers. Likely the men weren't passengers, anyway: guards probably, he reckoned. Then looked up sharply as Frank said,

'Ah, the hell with our square-off! I'll never have a better chance to nail you, Yance.'

The rifle swung in Yancey's direction. As he dived for the Colt he had dropped, he heard a shot and instinctively twisted aside. But didn't feel the expected bullet. Blinking, he looked up and saw Frank Greer lurch violently, his face a mess of gore. Then he was knocked flying as a second bullet took him in the chest and he dropped, thrashed briefly, dying with his eyes wide open in an incredulous stare.

A palefaced Jason Groom was on one knee, beside the splintered wreck of the coach, clutching a smoking carbine that he had obviously taken from one of the injured guards. He saw Yancey looking at him, wiped a shaking hand across his dusty face and smiled faintly.

'Told you once I was a good shot with a rifle.'

'You were better than good, kid,' Wade said feelingly.

Walt had taken a beating but was all right. He allowed Mattie to work over his wounds with warm water, empurpled with Condy's crystals.

The stage was wrecked and everyone marvelled that no one had been really seriously injured. But the special bracket Cameron had built to hold the strongbox of gold had broken, pulled out of the coachwood. The ironbound box had bounced and skidded into the stone wall of the well with tremendous force. The impact had splintered the bolted-on band, ripping several inches away from the wood.

Mitch Danner, crouched over the box, turned, looking disappointed. 'Damn! Thought I might get me a look at some of that gold! Been totin' shipments of it for years an' never even seen what it looks like. But I can only see a couple of rusty old bolts in there that must've tore loose.'

Yancey was talking with Jason and suddenly stopped speaking. '*Rusty* bolts? *Inside* the box?'

'Yeah. Why?' asked Mitch.

'Seems queer. I'd expect 'em on the outside where they'd been screwed in, holding those bands, not inside . . . '

The guards exchanged glances, one saying, 'Ho-lee *Mo!*'

It took a lot of effort to get past all the iron strapping Cameron had used to strengthen the hardwood box: sledge-hammers, chisels, even full-length crowbars. A lot of sweat was lost before the box burst open and spilled out its contents of . . . old twisted horseshoes, bent and damaged bolts by the dozen, cast-offs from a smithy's forge.

'My God!' exclaimed Walt Dedman, allowing Mattie to wipe his face as he stared aghast at the now shattered strongbox. 'Where're Fiddlers Green's gold ingots?'

Yancey Wade smiled crookedly. 'Reckon

Josh Cameron got his retirement money after all!'

There was a stunned silence at his words.

'He could hide for ever with that much gold,' Walt observed slowly.

'Lucky stiff!' said Wes Toohey with feeling.

*   *   *

By sundown most of the wreckage had been cleared away; Conchita had somehow managed to feed all the guards and Mitch Danner, as well as the usual way station workers.

Yancey Wade sat on the steps, his hunched figure glowing ruddy in the sun's rays as he rolled a cigarette. He glanced up as Mattie sat down beside him and handed him a cup of coffee.

He nodded his thanks and sipped. The cup was half-empty before she asked quietly,

'What will you do now, Yancey?'

'Have to go to Arizona. See what

happened to Terry and make sure he has a decent resting place.'

She moved closer and said, haltingly, 'I — I think I'd like to come with you.'

He looked at her sharply, emptied the cup and smiled slowly into her face, golden in the evening glow.

'Be glad of your company.'

Mattie smiled, too.

THE END

We do hope that you have enjoyed reading this large print book.

Did you know that all of our titles are available for purchase?

We publish a wide range of high quality large print books including:
Romances, Mysteries, Classics
General Fiction
Non Fiction and Westerns

Special interest titles available in large print are:
The Little Oxford Dictionary
Music Book, Song Book
Hymn Book, Service Book

Also available from us courtesy of Oxford University Press:
Young Readers' Dictionary
(large print edition)
Young Readers' Thesaurus
(large print edition)

For further information or a free brochure, please contact us at:
Ulverscroft Large Print Books Ltd.,
The Green, Bradgate Road, Anstey,
Leicester, LE7 7FU, England.
Tel: (00 44) 0116 236 4325
Fax: (00 44) 0116 234 0205

Other titles in the
Linford Western Library:

THE DEVIL'S WORK

Paul Bedford

Marshal Rance Toller is locking up a pair of troublemakers when Angie Sutter, a homesteader from a nearby valley, arrives with the news that her husband was murdered that morning. Whilst Rance has qualms about heading out into the frozen wasteland, leaving only an ageing deputy to stand guard, he accompanies Angie to her cabin — to find not only Jacob Sutter's body, but also that of his neighbour, slain by the same weapon. Meanwhile, back at the jailhouse, the deputy is dead and the prisoners gone . . .

REBEL RAIDERS

John Dyson

A gang of former Confederate soldiers is robbing and killing its way across Kansas. Novice lawman Cass Clacy is sent out after them, but what chance does he have of outgunning such experienced fighters? When Sheriff Jim Clarke joins Cass in the chase, his main aim is a share of the reward. Together they penetrate deep into the heart of the Indian Nations, where Cass falls under the spell of the lovely Audrey — but can he save her from the clutches of the dangerous Josiah Baines?

THE COMANCHE FIGHTS AGAIN

D. M. Harrison

Mitch Bayfield, known as 'Broke', was kidnapped and raised as a Comanche. When, many years later, he looks for his kin, he finds himself unable to settle in either world and turns his back on them all. He is determined, however, to return and liberate Little Bluestem, another white captive. The two of them flee, with the Comanche hot on their trail — but they are about to tangle with a ruthless gang of bank robbers . . .